TAKEN
UNDER
FIRE

Paranormal Investigative Services
Book Three

Sheri Lyn
Cassidy K. O'Connor

In a city divided, Agents Maddox and Tristan must protect the paranormal, unearth the truth, and prevent darkness from claiming all.

In the aftermath of the devastating destruction that befell the city six months ago, an ominous shroud now looms over them. Paranormals are vanishing at an alarming rate. As fear and suspicion cloud the minds of the city's inhabitants, calls for drastic measures grow louder, igniting tensions between supernatural beings and humanity.

Maddox and Tristan receive a mysterious visitor who unveils a hidden truth: the supernatural realm they were told had been obliterated is not only intact but still has people living there. As the agents delve deeper into the enigma, they find themselves being threatened by an unknown opponent.

With the city teetering on the brink of an all-out war, the agents must act swiftly. They form an unprecedented alliance, uniting humans and paranormals in a new task force, breaking barriers that were once thought insurmountable.

Can they untangle the web of deception and find the missing paranormals before it's too late? Only time will tell if their courage and resilience will be enough to save the city and prevent a catastrophe that could alter the fate of both realms forever.

To our fans who've fallen in love with Maddox and Tristan, this one's for you.

CHAPTER
One

SIX MONTHS later

Maddox sat in Scarlet, staring at the storefront. He would rather do anything else than what was planned for the day.

Tristan patted Maddox's knee. "Sitting out here isn't going to delay anything."

Maddox groaned. "But look at all the lace and flowers."

Tristan winced. "Yeah, there is that, but this is important to Marta. She asked you to be here, so suck it up and let's go."

"Fine, but I want a milkshake after this."

"You know what they say, right?" Tristan grinned,

"My milkshake brings all the boys to the yard. I got you covered, boo."

Maddox grumbled as he got out and stomped his way toward the wedding shop. Marta, Silas, Tallie, and Quinn were already inside sitting on couches waiting for them.

Marta jumped up and hugged him. "I'm so excited you guys could come. I warned Vic not to call you in today. If he does, I'll know you convinced him to call in a fake case."

Maddox laid his hand over his chest, faking offense. "I would never do that. I'm the best man and you asked me to be here and you need your Man of Honor here, so you have us for the whole day." He shook hands with Silas before turning back to Marta. "I heard Tristan has to wear a dress since he's standing on your side?"

Tristan gasped. "Excuse me? I never agreed to that. I'll be the best damn man of honor there is, but I draw the line at wearing a dress."

"But we'd look so good in matching gowns. I'm sure we can get high heels to fit those giant feet of yours." Tallie smiled gleefully.

"I would slay any dress I wore, but my shoulders are too big. They wouldn't fit in the dress. Plus, I don't want to take attention away from Marta and Silas."

Maddox sighed. "I think your legs would look great in heels."

Tallie gagged. "Can you guys explore that together later... when you're alone?"

"Someone please explain to me how she is such a prude? It makes no sense."

Marta shook her head at them. "She's not. She just knows she can get a rise out of you guys. And we've decided to have Tallie and Quinn on my side and the two of you on Silas side. Crisis averted."

A woman walked out of a back room with several dresses slung over her arm. "If everyone is here now, we can get started. Marta, I'll put these in this room for you. And Silas, I have a few tuxes in that room for you. Everyone else can have a seat while they do a fashion show for us."

Quinn raised her hand and spoke quietly. "They can't see each other in their wedding attire before the ceremony. Do you have some kind of partition or something we can put between them?"

Everyone stared at the newly turned paranormal girl. Sometimes Maddox forgot how stringent humans were.

Marta shook her head. "But honey, we've been together for years."

Quinn shook her head. "I don't care how old you are. This is your first wedding, so we are doing this right."

Maddox's eyebrows rose halfway up his forehead. That was the most forceful the girl had been since coming to live with Marta and Tallie six months ago.

"It's bad luck for the groom to see the dress before the wedding." Tristan agreed with a nod to Quinn. "And come on, it took you guys this long to get to this point. Do you really want to take any chance of jinxing shit?"

Silas stepped into the tiny dressing room. "While we're getting ready, you guys can solve the partition issue."

The older couple disappeared behind their curtains. The wedding planner turned to them helplessly. "I don't have a fake wall to put up."

"What about that?" Tallie pointed at a large sign across the room.

The wedding planner's shoulders dropped. "Just be careful."

Maddox and Tristan walked over and picked up the large wooden sign decorated with flowers that said 'She said yes to the dress' and walked it over between the dressing rooms.

Maddox walked back and sat on the couch. "Is everyone satisfied now?"

Quinn nodded happily.

A squeal from Marta's room had everyone looking her way. "Could someone help me? These buttons and zippers are absolutely ridiculous."

Everyone turned and looked at Maddox. "No way. Tallie, you've been with her for almost a year. You're up."

She rolled her eyes at him. "Who's the prude now?"

She disappeared behind the curtain.

Silas walked out and paraded in a solid white tux. "This is kind of snazzy."

Maddox and Tristan shook their heads at the same time. "You look like you're working the gates of heaven."

Silas chuckled as he went back behind the curtain.

Marta came out next. Quinn wolf-whistled. "Holy crap."

Maddox shook his head violently. "Absolutely not."

Tallie scowled at him. "She looks gorgeous. Look at the cleavage this corset is giving her."

Marta squeezed Tallie's hand. "I sort of feel like a high-end escort. I can't breathe. But I do agree my boobs look fantastic."

Maddox groaned. "Gross."

"You do look fabulous, though." Tristan agreed, "But yeah, I don't think it's right for this occasion."

The two women went back to their room.

Silas walked out with his arms spread wide. "This is nice."

The black pants and purple velvet jacket did look good on him but... "Um... not sure that's proper wedding attire." He leaned close to Tristan. "What the hell was this wedding planner thinking? They aren't twenty and this isn't Vegas."

Quinn snorted. "Mr. Silas, you look fantastic, but no, I am vetoing this one."

The fae dropped his shoulders and slunk back to his waiting room.

Marta walked out waving her hand like the Queen in a parade. The gown was made almost entirely of peacock feathers. The massive feathers of a peacock's tail were spread out behind her head and shoulders.

"Oh my god. How many peacock shifters died to make that?" Maddox's eyes bulged.

Tallie sneezed. "I'm vetoing this one. It's making me itch just being near it."

"*That's* the only reason you're saying no?" Tristan asked skeptically. "Maybe we should try a different shop... I'm starting to question this ladies' fashion sense."

Maddox and Quinn nodded in agreement.

A few minutes later, Marta and Silas walked out at the same time. Quinn gasped. "You guys look perfect."

Maddox couldn't find anything wrong with the ice blue beaded gown Marta had on and the slate gray tux Silas wore.

"Woah, holy hell, that's hot." Tristan grimaced as Maddox shot him a look. "I mean, they complement each other so perfectly."

The wedding coordinator clapped her hands together. "Excellent choices. Let me pull some gowns and tuxes to match these for the wedding party, and you guys can go next."

Tristan raised his hand to get her attention. "Can we buy one of those suits for Maddox? Not for the wedding, but just because..." He bit his lip and made a show of looking Maddox up and down.

Once the dressing rooms were reset for them, Maddox and Tristan went behind the curtain. Maddox huffed. "I was really hoping the lady would have put a dress in here for you. I'm really liking the image in my head right now." He sighed as he pulled the pants off the hanger. "Let's get this over with."

They changed quickly and walked out while everyone was looking at Tallie and Quinn in their dresses.

Marta's hand came to her chest when she saw them. "You both look so handsome." Tears welled in her eyes. "I hope one day soon we'll be doing this for your wedding."

Maddox's jaw dropped. "Really Mom? It's only been a few months. Don't put Tristan on the spot like that."

Tristan raised his eyebrow at Maddox, "Um... who's the commitment phobe here?"

Maddox had no doubt Tristan was the man for him. As soon as possible he wanted to marry him but humans did everything slower than shifters since they didn't have the true mate thing so he wasn't going to rush Tristan. Like Quinn, they had a lot of human norms to forget about.

Silas tapped his chin. "I do say this is going to be the best looking wedding party in history." He reached over and grabbed Marta's hand, bringing it to his lips and kissing her. "You'll be the most dazzling of all. I can't wait to see you coming down the aisle."

Maddox was shocked to see tears in his dad's eyes. Silas really did love Marta, didn't he? Maddox glanced over at Tristan and squeezed his hand. He was so damn happy for his mom and for himself. They were finally getting the happily ever after they both deserved.

The wedding planner clapped her hands. "If everyone is happy, we can get started on the cake testing. I admit your list of flavors to try was longer than usual, but I think you'll be pleased with everything."

Marta scrunched her eyebrows together. "I only sent three flavors."

Silas pursed his lips. "I may have sent a couple."

One by one, they all admitted to adding to the list. Marta should never have given them all access to the wedding planning software.

Marta chuckled. "I guess it's a good thing I wore a loose-fitting dress. Let's go try these concoctions you all came up with."

The group changed back into their regular

clothes and followed the wedding planner to a side room with a buffet of small cakes displayed.

"If everyone would like to take a seat," she motioned to the table set up for a fancy tea party. "Next to your plates are a sheet of paper and a pen. As you taste each cake, you can give it a score or write your thoughts about it. At the end, we can compare notes and hopefully decide on a flavor or flavors, depending on how many layers you want."

The young assistant bounced on her toes. "I, for one, can't wait to hear your thoughts. These are definitely some of the most unique combinations we've been asked to create."

"We'll start with the more traditional flavors." The two women cut up the first cake and walked around with small plates. "This first one is carrot cake with cream cheese icing."

Everyone took small bites and made their notes.

"Next is a chocolate cake with fudge icing."

Tallie danced in her seat. "This was my suggestion."

They repeated the process for a red velvet cake, which Quinn said was her suggestion.

The assistant giggled. "Now for the fun ones."

First up was a ginger cardamom cake with rose buttercream. Then a Pistachio and rose cake with

Italian buttercream which half the group spit out into napkins. The lavender cake with rose icing tasted like an actual flower, which was not pleasant. The matcha cake with dark chocolate frosting tasted like grass to Maddox. The pumpkin cake with maple cinnamon frosting was a surprising flavor, but seemed weird for a wedding. Last was a lemon elderflower cake with elderflower frosting.

Silas rubbed his hands together eagerly. "I can't wait for this one. It was my favorite cake growing up." He looked at Maddox. "Your grandmother would make it for my birthday every year."

Maddox nodded, but didn't say anything. He realized how little he knew about his dad's side of the family. He'd never met his grandmother. She'd passed away before he was born. One day soon, he'd have to sit with his dad and hear his life story. What else did he not know about him?

The wedding planner passed out coffee and tea. "Now let's start easy. I'll say a cake and raise your hand if you are voting for it. This will make it easy to see if any flavors are unanimously voted out. But remember, in the end, the bride and groom are making the final decision." She gave them each a mom stare before starting. "How many votes for red velvet?" Everyone raised their hand. One by one, she went down the list. The only cake no one raised their hand for was the lavender cake with rose icing. No one admitted who had put it on the list either.

"Okay, now we narrow it down. Remember, we can make each layer a different flavor so it's really up to you how big you want the cake."

All at once, everyone spoke at the same time. Each pitched their case for the flavors they liked.

In the end, they decided on a bottom layer of red velvet, a middle layer of pumpkin cake, and a top layer of lemon elderflower. The cake for the bridal shower would be chocolate with fudge icing, and the rehearsal dinner cake would be the carrot cake.

Marta leaned back and took a deep breath. "I still don't see why we are doing all these parties and rehearsals. Why can't we just do it in the backyard?"

Silas grabbed her hand. "We will do whatever you want but when we first planned this everyone agreed you deserved an extravagant gala and part of you agreed you thought it sounded romantic. If you want to change anything, there is still time. I want to give you everything you want. I've waited a long time for you to give in and let me spoil you."

Marta blushed at his words. "You are too good to me."

He leaned over and kissed her forehead. "I'm just getting started."

Maddox heard the other four women in the room sigh. He wasn't sure, but he may have heard Tristan sigh too. He really needed to up his game. His dad was seriously romantic and eloquent. Maddox wanted to be that for Tristan too.

CHAPTER
Two

TRISTAN DROPPED into a chair at the conference table and laid his head down with a sigh. "Why did we have to do this so early?"

"It's nine a.m., that's not early." Sheppard laughed. "Rough night?"

"I ran out of coffee at home and he-" Tristan threw his hand out and pointed to Maddox. "-wouldn't stop on the way in because he didn't want to risk Scarlet. My boyfriend is so mean to me, guys."

"There is perfectly good coffee here. You don't need to risk burning Scarlet."

Tristan rolled his eyes. "Like I'd waste any of the manna of the gods by spilling it." He grumbled as he stood up and headed out of the room. "Don't start without me. I'll be right back."

He beelined for the kitchen and the coffee that awaited him there. It wasn't as good as he could get at home, but it was still caffeine. Within minutes, he'd prepared two large cups and headed back to the meeting.

"Now that everyone is here," Vic announced with a pointed look at Tristan.

Tristan smiled as he carefully sat down and placed his cups on the table. "This was life or death, I swear. You don't want me to interact with people without it. Especially people that don't know me yet."

Half the room nodded in agreement, which made Tristan frown at them. Yeah, he'd said it, but they didn't need to agree so readily.

"Anyway, for those of you who I haven't officially met in person, I'm ASAC Victor Judge and this is the first official meeting of the newly formed joint task force for TPD and P.I.S.." Vic made eye contact with everyone in the room, "You were chosen because somebody recommended you to join this group. You've all proven you are willing to work with us without prejudice."

Tristan raised his hand to get Vic's attention.

"Yes?" Vic asked with a sigh.

"Just to clarify, what is our main purpose?"

"You can just sit there and drink your coffee and let me get through this and then we'll get to that part."

Tristan shrugged, "Sorry, didn't mean to jump ahead. I got excited, I guess."

"For now, the agency has decided my team and you five humans will be the test group. If we're successful, they'll expand to the other field offices. That means we have a lot of pressure on us. If any of you aren't up to it, you're free to walk away with no judgment from us."

Tristan glanced from face to face to see how the non-supes were taking Vic's words. He recognized most of them and knew they were good people.

When no one made a move to leave or speak, Vic nodded. "As of this morning, you've all been assigned to this office as long as the task force exists. You're essentially now employed by P.I.S.."

The humans mumbled amongst themselves for a moment, but quickly died down as Vic waited patiently for them to come to terms with their new employment.

"My pod is split into teams of two. The humans will be split among them. This is," Vic pointed to Cole sitting to his right, "Cole Brendel, Koala Shifter. He's our tech genius and next to him is his partner,

Reed Gentry. He's an Amarok and has a photographic memory."

"Jaylen, you'll be paired up with them. For those of you who don't know, Jaylen Rose helped us solve a case and is one of the reasons we pushed for this task force to begin with. With his help, we found a connection between a TPD case and ours, which helped stop a lot of kids from going missing."

Jaylen stood up with a smile and moved to sit next to his new team. "Hey, guys."

Vic gave them a minute to exchange greetings and then pointed at the next team. "Raelle Dawson, Siren, she's a master at interrogation, and her partner, Cross Hawkins. He's a wyvern and a skilled hostage negotiator. Derek Vickers, you'll be with them."

Derek stood and moved to the open seat next to them with a tentative smile.

Tristan nodded as the kid met his eyes from across the table. That would be a good match. They'd take good care of him and teach him all he needed to know. If Raelle didn't scare him off with her flirting, that was.

"Okay, next we have Jasmina Love, Unicorn, but don't let that fool you. She's also the team's sharpshooter." He grinned at Jasmina's laugh and pointed to Kiely. "She's partnered with Kiely Black. She's an empath and our behavior specialist, and if that wasn't enough, she's a Pegasus."

"Who's the lucky winner to join our team?" Kiely asked eagerly.

"Lexi Brooks."

The woman stood with a smile and offered her hand. "It's a pleasure to join your team. I look forward to working with you both."

"Ensley Hanson is a Seer and next to her is Sheppard Wilder, Vampire, and weapons expert." Vic paused and studied Ensley. "Be on your best behavior, and don't scare off your new team member, agreed?"

Ensley frowned. "Really? You act like I'm the worst of this group."

Vic grumbled and turned. "Willow Parks, you're with them. If you have any issues, let me know."

Tristan grinned and turned to his old friend, "Josh, that means you're with us."

"You couldn't let me finish, could you?" Vic grumbled, "Everybody, this is Tristan James, phoenix shifter and all-around pain in my ass, and his partner, the bigger pain in my ass, Maddox Smith. He's our linguist and half fae, half-ogre. Joshua Bradley is joining their team. I'll give everyone a few minutes to get acquainted, then we'll get the actual meeting started."

The groups all turned to each other and started talking at the same time.

Josh smiled at Maddox and Tristan. "This is the biggest pay jump I've ever gotten. Maybe it does pay to not play politics."

Tristan slapped him on the back. "I'm glad we were able to steal you away. You were being wasted in that department."

Vic came back into the room and tossed a large stack of folders on the table. "Okay, this is why we're here. Some details of Quinn Roger's case leaked and now people know paranormal parts can heal humans. As you've all seen over the last few months, cases are opened every day of paranormals being taken and new underground organ markets are popping up everywhere. The U.S. government is working fast to establish ethical, legal ways for paranormals to donate to humans, hoping it slows down the illegal bullshit. Not to mention the growing section of the human population that take both Tristan and Quinn's transitions as attacks on their kind so crime between the two groups is on the rise too."

He separated the folders into five small stacks

and walked around, setting a pile in front of each group. "As I said before, we are a test group and if it works out, they'll roll these teams out nationwide. Our lovely governor is, of course, doing everything he can to stop this. He wants our kind locked away, so having us getting along is the last thing he wants."

Mumbles echoed around the room.

"The F.B.I. said they've heard chatter about a black market that recently started up in this area. In our region, in the last six months, reports of missing paranormals have risen over forty percent. Each one of these files represents one case. We'll need to verify the information and, with any luck, knock some of these names off our list of potential victims."

Tristan counted their files and then looked at the stack in front of the rest of the group. "Holy shit, that's a lot of people that have gone missing. Why are we just now looking into this?"

"They were initially looked into, but they all went cold. No bodies have turned up and no evidence to lead anyone to believe they'd been taken by force." Vic sighed and shrugged. "I'm not going to lie. We've got shit to go on. Word is spreading about the number of disappearances and paranormals are putting pressure on their elected officials to do something. We're sitting on a ticking time bomb here and with the tension rising between humans and supes, we have to walk a fine line."

Maddox sighed. "Why can't we live and let live? I have no doubt there are plenty of paranormals that would help humans in a safe way. I'm so tired of this us and them mentality."

Vic nodded. "And that's why we have this task force. Together we can do so much more, and we're going to prove that to the world."

Ensley pulled her stack toward her. "You gave me the most interesting cases, right?"

Tristan laughed and then stood up with a look at her new human team member. "Good luck with her. You're going to need it."

She scoffed at him. "Come on, I haven't had a gory body in a long time. Everything has been so mundane. Where are all the crazies?"

"In your family tree, maybe?" Maddox joked.

She pretended to think for a second. "I do have some lingering questions about my uncle, so you never know."

Vic rolled his eyes. "Ensley, behave. You've got your assignments, get to work, and report in as you find anything."

CHAPTER
Three

MADDOX OPENED the door to their tiny office and waved to a small table in the corner. "This is where you'll be working. The laptop is already set up for you. When you first log in, it will ask you to create a new password. It's going to be cozy in here, but maybe if the task force works out, they'll build us bigger offices."

He tossed the files down and grabbed the top one as he sat down. "I guess we each take one and get up to speed." He flipped open his file. "I'm going to look into Sheila Bates."

Josh grabbed a file and scanned it. "I've got Raul Lopez."

Tristan grabbed the next one in the pile, "And unlucky contestant number three is Jeffrey Barnes."

Maddox hopped up and wrote the three names on the whiteboard. Josh grabbed the other two and glanced at them. "Next will be Antonio Mancini and Maria Vasquez."

Maddox nodded as he added them. "Let's see if we can get all the interviews scheduled for this week, if possible. As you get a time scheduled write it on the board so we don't double book ourselves."

The room was quiet as each of them studied the files and researched their victims in the various databases.

Tristan hung up the phone and moved to the board. "We've got an interview for this afternoon with Barnes' sister. She'll meet us at his home."

"Nice. I'm calling my vic's neighbor now. I'll see if she's available tomorrow." Maddox said as he dialed the number into his phone.

While he talked with Mrs. Hansen, he saw Josh get up and go to the whiteboard and write Tuesday 2 p.m. next to Raul's name.

He hung up and wrote Tuesday eleven a.m. next to Maria's name. He turned back to grab another file, but Tristan and Josh had taken the remaining two. "Guess I'll grab coffee for everyone. Let's get those last two scheduled, then we can get to the Barnes' place."

The outer pod area was silent as everyone was focused on their computers. It was good to see the humans sitting side by side with them, not even blinking that they were surrounded by paranormals.

He made three cups of coffee and brought them back. "So how'd we do?"

Josh pointed at the board. "We're going to see Maria's roommate Wednesday at four at the University of Tampa campus library."

"I talked to Antonio's Agent. He can't meet us till the end of the week at the earliest as he's out of town with one of his clients at a shoot. He should be back on Friday and can meet us that afternoon. He'll call Thursday to give us a time, though." Tristan took the cup of coffee with a sigh of happiness.

"Look at us. Working like a well-oiled machine already. Let's get on the road so we're not late."

"No," Tristan whined as he held up his cup. "I haven't even gotten to take more than a sip. You can't be this cruel to bring us coffee and then say leave it behind."

Maddox lifted one eyebrow at him. "Who said anything about leaving it behind? Josh won't be comfortable in the backseat of Scarlet, so we're taking your truck. I don't mind drinking in there, do you?"

"Oh." Tristan laughed. "Not at all. I don't treat my truck as if it's a goddess unfit for mere mortal bodies to touch."

"I don't blame Maddox. If I had that car, I would be the same way." Josh added as he took the coffee and walked toward the door.

"Oh, for fuck's sake, don't encourage him. Do you know how hard he is to live with now? I swear he loves that machine more than he will ever love me."

The drive to Hyde Park didn't take long. They went up to apartment 403 and knocked. A young woman answered the door. She had deep bags under her eyes, as if she hadn't slept in days.

"Afternoon. I'm Debbie. Come on in." She stepped back and let them file in. "There's a lot more of you this time. Should I take that as a good sign?"

They held up their badges. "I'm Senior Special Agent Maddox Smith. This is my partner, Special Agent Tristan James. This is Officer Joshua Bradley. He's a liaison from the Tampa P.D. Why don't we have a seat?"

She led them to the small living room and sat in the recliner while the three of them squished onto the couch.

Tristan giggled as he wiggled his ass, trying to get more comfortable in between the two larger men. "My balls are getting squished," He whispered.

Maddox bit his lip to keep from laughing. "We understand your brother has been missing for four months now and there hasn't been any activity on his social media or financial accounts. Our team was recently assigned his case so it would have fresh eyes on it. Would you mind taking us through the last time you saw him?"

Debbie nodded. "Our parents have been gone for a few years, so it's just me and Jeff. I usually talk to him twice a week. Everything seemed fine leading up to his disappearance. His co-workers said he was normal at work and when he left that Friday he was smiling and happy."

"Was he seeing anyone at the time?"

She shook her head. "He went on dates, but nothing serious for a while now." She paused and looked around the apartment. "I have to pack this place up soon. His lease is up and I can't afford to keep it while I wait for him to come back."

Maddox didn't want to give the girl any hope. After this long with complete silence, it wasn't likely he was just going to waltz in the door like he was on vacation. "Do you mind if my partners here have a look around?"

She waved her hand above her head. "Sure. Anything that helps."

Tristan and Josh got up and went through the two doors across the room.

Maddox pulled out his notepad. "What hobbies did Mr. Barnes have? Was there anywhere he frequented often? A usual place he went to meet up with dates?"

"This area always has stuff going on. He did a lot of trivia nights at the bars around here. I don't know of a specific place he went to meet women. Like everyone our age, it's either out at a bar or on a dating app. I can give you his laptop if that helps. I know your people already went through it once, but maybe you'll see something they didn't. His phone was never found and the phone company said it hasn't been active since the night he disappeared."

Tristan stuck his head out of the room he was in. "I saw in the file reports about their findings, but a second look might not be a bad idea."

Maddox stood up and held his hand out. "We appreciate you taking the time to talk to us. We're going to go back through everything and we'll keep you updated on any developments. Here's my card if anything comes up in the meantime."

She took the card and set it on the kitchen

counter, then handed him the laptop. "I'm glad you guys haven't given up on him yet."

She walked the group out and locked up behind them.

They didn't speak again until they were back in the truck. "So, did you guys see anything of note in the other rooms?"

Tristan smirked, "Well, he likes to have fun in the bedroom, but nothing of importance, really. Just run of the mill kinky stuff, and it might have given me a few ideas for our room too."

Josh rolled his eyes. "Haven't you heard 'don't kiss and tell'?"

"I'm not telling anything, just stating a fact." Tristan winked. "Did you find anything of interest or are you going to keep giving me shit?"

"Nope, nothing really. Well, he did have a special order shampoo for balding. Kind of ironic, considering he was a wolf shifter."

Maddox threw back his head and laughed. "Oh my god. I'm trying to imagine a bald wolf running around. That would look so creepy."

"If they sat down in their animal form, would they leave those butt prints like hairless cats do?" Tristan questioned.

Josh made a gagging noise from the backseat.

Maddox pulled out his phone and looked at the time. "It's only four, but I say we go to Froggy's and have a celebratory first day drink."

"I'll text the rest of the team with an open invite in case anyone wants to join us," Tristan said as he pulled out his phone.

Maddox glanced over his shoulder at Josh. "Are you good with going into a supe bar? I promise no one will bother you and the bartender is totally cool with us bringing humans in."

Josh looked a little pale, but he shrugged. "I'm game for a new experience. What's the worst that can happen?"

CHAPTER
Four

TRISTAN PULLED open the door to Froggy's and waved for Josh and Maddox to go in first. He patted Josh's back as he went by. "You'll love Froggy. Just don't let him give you one of the supe drinks. Trust me on that."

Josh nodded hesitantly. "Maybe I shouldn't drink at all, just in case."

"No way. We're here to celebrate our partnership, you have to drink to that. And besides, Maddox here can take care of us. He's got lots of experience doing it." Tristan winked at his boyfriend as he waved to Froggy.

Maddox groaned. "When did I become the babysitter of sloppy drunks?"

Tristan moved to lean against the bar as he

laughed at Maddox. "Froggy, meet our new partner, Josh. Josh, this is the best bartender in all of Tampa, and he can carry your ass out of here if he needed to. He's that strong."

"We invited the rest of the team too, and they're bringing their new human partners. Hope that's okay?" Maddox asked as he pushed the bowl of mixed nuts far away from him.

"If they're cool, I'm cool." Froggy agreed easily. "The most important question is what am I supposed to give them to drink? It's not like I carry human-grade shit here, you know."

"What if you watered it down?" Josh asked with a curious frown. "Is supe alcohol really that much stronger, though?"

All three men nodded their heads. "Tristan got so wasted, we had to carry him out of here. And that's not to mention Jaylen."

Froggy laughed. "I think Jaylen held it better than your boy did, though."

The door swung open as the rest of the team filed in. The other bar patrons were giving weary glances at the humans, but they knew better than to challenge the agents.

Froggy held up his hands in surrender. "Don't even try to introduce everybody to me at once. If you come back, I'll get to know you, and don't take that as if you're not welcome. Just if you can handle the alcohol and the shit-talking from this group and want to come back." He shrugged and trailed off with a sheepish look at Maddox and Tristan. "I'm fucking rambling, aren't I?"

Maddox and Tristan nodded with shit-eating grins on their faces.

He flicked them off. "Go sit down. I'll bring your usuals to you."

Tristan laughed as he followed the group to a set of tables as they rearranged them so they could all sit together.

"So, how was everyone's first day as a new team?" Maddox asked.

Jaylen laughed as he took a seat. "Wasn't that much different for me, but I'm used to you guys and how you do things. Though I've got to say working as part of the task force is so much better than just being a liaison."

"I don't have much to compare it to," Derek interjected. "I'm only a rookie, so everything is exciting and new for me."

"I don't know about the rest of you, but I really enjoyed the interview part of the process. Humans are a little intimidated by cops, but damn, walk in as a P.I.S. agent and you automatically get respect from everyone. Badass." Lexi bumped her shoulder into Kieley's.

"Awe shucks. We enjoy the badassness of it too." Kiely shot back.

Willow brushed her hair off her shoulder. "Well, we closed one of our cases already. Dude was fine, just went on a bender and is back with his family now. They forgot to call and close the case."

Tristan groaned, "So that only leaves us with twenty-eight more."

"Okay, so these are the supe drinks, and this tray is for the humans. Take it easy, 'cause I'm not sure if they're gonna be too strong still or not." Froggy said as he gestured to the assortment. "If this is going to be a regular thing, I'll start stocking some human-grade shit for you all."

Tristan grabbed a mug of cold beer and raised it. "A toast to us and the future. May this be the start of a new dynasty."

Maddox nodded. "We are making history here. Let's work our asses off and show the rest of the world our kinds can work together."

"I agree," Ensley added. "Getting to work on human cases would be all new bodies and creepers to bust."

Everyone groaned and shook their heads at her.

Tristan laughed, "To us," and then he took a long drink, nearly draining the glass. "Now let's have some fun, but remember children, tomorrow is a workday and you don't want to piss off Vic or grumpy ass over here."

Maddox lifted one eyebrow. "Just because some of us take our job seriously doesn't mean we are grumpy."

"Babe, I live with you. You are grumpy in the mornings, and if you don't get fed quick enough and..." Tristan grinned as everyone around the table laughed.

"Hey Froggy, turn that up." A shifter in the corner yelled over the crowd.

Everyone turned to see what was on the tv that had him interrupting everyone.

A breaking news alert graphic splashed across the screen. The anchor came on without his usual smile and chipper attitude. "Senator Richard Crump has just announced a new bill he is proposing which will require all supernaturals to be micro-chipped and tracked. He will hold a press conference momentarily." The anchor paused. "And we're going live to that conference."

Everyone jumped up from their seats and

crowded around the bar in front of the t.v. The senator walked on the screen and stood behind a podium. Flashes of light erupted around the room. He held his hands up to quiet everyone. "Good evening. Many years ago we were invaded by these creatures and told we have to live side by side with them. We tried doing that. And what happened? They are killing us, destroying our cities, and changing our humans to be abominations like them. It's time we took back control of our cities and our lives. I'm proposing a bill that will require all non-humans to be micro-chipped and monitored like the animals they are. We'll build fenced-in cities to keep them contained and away from the good people of Florida and the rest of the country. Thank you for your time."

The video cut back to the anchor in the news-room. His face said it all. The look of disgust and anger was clear to see. "I'm struggling to come up with words. We're going to cut to a commercial break."

"Holy shit," Tristan whispered as he glanced around the room in a shocked stupor. "Did that really just happen?"

Cole nodded as he typed away on his phone, "It's

already all over the internet. They're calling for protests. Things are going to get ugly quick."

Josh swallowed as he moved to sit back at the table. "Why do I suddenly feel like this task force just got a target on its back?"

"Maybe not a target." Tristan winced, "But we're going to get a hell of a lot of scrutiny from both sides for a while, that's for sure."

Maddox pulled his phone out of his pocket. "Vic just texted the higher-ups are already talking and making plans. He wants everyone in at eight a.m. sharp to discuss."

Cross took his drink and shot it back in one gulp. "I guess we better cut this short since we have to be in early."

Tristan nodded sadly. "Fucking hell, all we wanted was one night to celebrate the huge step forward we'd taken by creating this team, and then this had to happen."

The team expressed their agreement, said their goodbyes, and headed out. "Come on Josh, we can drop you off at headquarters, or depending on where you live, we can just take you home and pick you up on the way in the morning."

Josh threw cash down on the table. "Best you

guys don't drive in my neighborhood after that news. You can just drop me at my car."

Maddox nodded solemnly. "This is so fucked up. I never imagined something like this being a possibility. I didn't think there was that much hatred of our kind."

Josh held the door of the bar open to let them walk out first. "Not all humans think like Senator Dick there. I can't imagine this will actually pass, but it's sure going to cause a lot of problems."

CHAPTER
Five

MADDOX AND TRISTAN walked into the pod and nodded to the rest of the team as they took their seats and turned to face Vic who stood at the head of the table with a look of resignation on his face. He looked as if he'd aged ten years since they'd seen him the day before.

"Did you get any sleep last night?" Tristan asked.

Vic shrugged. "Probably about as much as any of you did."

"So, do we have a plan of action? Did the higher-ups give any orders?" Maddox asked.

"We're going to continue working on the cases we were given. Since this senator is from Florida, we expect a lot of the protests and shit to happen here.

Everyone is on standby to respond to riots and any other bullshit that's going to come from all this."

Tristan raised his hand. "What does this mean for the task force?"

Vic leaned back, pulling his shoulders straight. He looked at them one by one as he talked. "Absolutely nothing changes. We are going to show everyone our kinds can work together. There are enough decent humans in the Senate that I think this will get struck down. We are going to continue doing our jobs as long as we are able to. Now get back to work, but keep your phones nearby at all times. If you're in the field and run into any issues, call for backup. Look out for each other."

Maddox knocked on the table. "We're heading out. We have an interview set for eleven. Call us if you need us."

The trio made their way downstairs to Tristan's truck. He put the address to the Pine Valley Retirement community where their victim, Sheila Bates lived. As they drove through the streets, it had already transformed overnight. Small groups of people stood on corners with signs either supporting or hating the new proposal. You could feel the tension in the air. The city felt like it was going to erupt at any minute.

They parked in a guest spot and checked in at the receptionist's desk. The young woman called the property manager to escort them to the victim's apartment.

The woman came out a few minutes later and led them back out front to a golf cart. "Our property is on a hundred acres, so it's easier to travel this way."

As they drove through the area, people stopped what they were doing to wave at them. They passed a large pool with mermaids, dolphins, and a couple of otters swimming. On the other side of the road, a group of trolls were playing shuffleboard.

Maddox couldn't imagine living in a place like this. He liked his independence too much. This felt like forced interaction. "Is this one of those places where everyone knows everyone and their business, too?"

The woman's eyes bulged as she nodded. "It's crazy how bad it is. There is always drama and people butting in where they shouldn't. It's worse than high school, really."

"This place is like no community I've ever been in," Josh said as his head swiveled back and forth, taking it all in.

Tristan snickered as he took in the people, "Is

this place anything like the one in North Florida, with all the color-coded loofahs?"

Maddox made a disgusted look. "Do I even want to know what the hell you're talking about?"

The property manager cringed, "It's basically a system they set up for swinging I guess you'd say."

Tristan nodded, "I can't believe you haven't heard of The Villages. Everyone knows about it. Have you been living under a rock?"

Maddox shrugged. "I guess it's a human thing. Supes don't care about nudity and things like that. I don't think we really need a color-coded system. Most of our kinds have true mates, so swinging isn't much of a thing. For those that don't do mates, they just say who or what they want, and if the other person is into it, they go for it. Humans can be so weird and prudish."

Everyone nodded their agreement.

The manager pulled the cart to a stop in front of a three-story building. "Sheila lived on the third floor. She had no family and her apartment was fully paid off, so we're keeping it until she is either found or declared dead."

"Who reported her missing?" Tristan climbed out of the cart and glanced around, taking in all the faces watching them.

"As you can see, nothing goes unnoticed around here for long. Sheila doesn't have any family and in the years she's lived here, she's never had anyone come to stay, even for a night. So when it was brought to our attention that she hadn't come home all night, we were concerned. After two days with no word, I reported it to the police."

She unlocked the apartment and let them enter. It was as drab and boring as Maddox had imagined it would be. Everything was in place. The report said there was no sign of foul play or forced entry. They did note the neighbors reported many of the victim's personal belongings like photo albums and her prized Disney ceramic houses collection were missing.

The three of them fanned out and went room by room and verified everything the report had said.

"Um, guys, can you guys come in here?" Josh called out from a room down the hall.

They gathered in the doorway, surprised at what they saw. Instead of a normal bedroom with furniture, it was a giant sandbox with miniature exercise equipment spread around.

"I know I'm new to all of this, but this seems like some kinky stuff," Josh whispered to them.

The office manager giggled. "It's not what you

think. Sheila was a gopher shifter and didn't like working out with the larger animals. She created her own home gym. Nothing sexual here." She gave him a small wink.

His cheeks reddened at being overheard.

Maddox shrugged and went back out into the living room. "It's been four months. No one has heard from her at all, correct?"

She nodded. "No news at all. Georgina down the hall even tried tracking down any extended family members but couldn't find anyone."

Maddox nodded and exited into the hallway. "Let's split up and interview everyone on this floor." He turned to their escort. "If there is anyone else on the property she was close with, can you bring them here?"

"Sheila was nice, but not super outgoing. She pretty much just hung out with her neighbors."

He thanked her and moved down to the door furthest down the hall. With only eight doors and one of those being the victim's it shouldn't take them all that long. They could be done in time to grab lunch before their next interview.

CHAPTER
Six

TRISTAN GROANED as he pulled himself up into his truck. "That was so good, but why did you let me eat so much?"

"We told you to stop, but you don't listen," Josh argued from the back seat. "You were too busy moaning over the taste. It was kind of obscene at times, actually."

Tristan flipped him off.

Maddox shrugged. "I personally loved the moans."

"Thanks, babe," Tristan replied with a grin as he typed in the address to the next interview. "So next up we have Raul Lopez. He's forty-five and married. His wife reported him missing when he didn't return home from a business trip."

"Shit," Maddox exclaimed as he slammed on the brakes.

"What the hell is that?" Josh pointed to the barricades lining the street. "Are they seriously segregating the damn roads now?"

Tristan frowned as he took in both sides of the road, and the people standing there screaming at each other. "Should we be grateful they are staying separated for the moment?"

"Should we call this in?" Josh questioned.

"You call it in. I'll move the barricade so we can get by." Tristan opened his door and the jeers and insults became louder. He winced at some of the vile words they were tossing at each other. When had humanity fallen so far that it was okay to treat each other like this?

Maddox grabbed one end of the wood plank closest to him and pulled it off the pile of junk they'd built up between them. He spun around when something hit him in the center of his back. His wings immediately popped out. Ready to fight whatever violence was coming his way. A can of peaches was sitting at his feet.

"Who the fuck threw that?" Tristan demanded as he stared down both sides of the street, daring someone to admit it. He could feel his anger building the more he thought about Maddox getting hit for doing his job.

"He's a fucking abomination. Look at those dainty wings on that huge ass body."

Tristan felt his body burn as his wings popped out. He could see wisps of smoke curling from his arms and body. Part of him was freaked out, but the rest of him was focused on keeping his mate safe from whatever danger lurked close by.

The fear on the human's faces was obvious, but most stood their ground.

Josh got between them and held up a can of pepper spray. "Anyone still here in thirty seconds is going to get sprayed."

Both sides of the road quickly dispersed.

Maddox grabbed Tristan's arm and spun him toward him. "I have never been so turned on in my life. Look at your fucking wings. They're on literal fire. And you were ready to tear those people up."

Josh cleared his throat. "This may not be the best place for this. You two look ready to tear each other's clothes off, and I'm not sure the crowds can handle that right now."

Tristan laughed as he stepped back from Maddox, "So now that I'm hot and bothered in more than one way, can anyone tell me how to turn them off? My truck may not be Scarlet, but I still don't want to burn the interior."

Both men shrugged.

"I could try slapping your ass, but somehow I don't think that will do it." Maddox unhelpfully offered.

Josh groaned. "No kinky shit in public, boys."

Tristan laughed as he felt some of the tension slowly leave his body. Within a few minutes, he could feel his core temperature dropping too. He glanced over his shoulder to see his wings. "Okay, so I think I got this."

It took another minute, but he was able to finally make his wings retract so they could finish removing the debris pile and get on their way.

It took them almost half an hour, but they finally were able to clear the road. They were careful to keep an eye out for any resurgence of the crowd. As they climbed back into the truck, Tristan let out a loud sigh. "I'd like to say things can't get any worse, but I know this was only the tip of the iceberg. Is it too late to retire to some uninhabited island somewhere?"

Josh and Maddox murmured their agreement.

The rest of the trip to Raul's house was uneventful. As they pulled up to the home inside the

Bayshore Beautiful neighborhood, Tristan whistled. "This is a really nice area to live in, with the market the way it is. I can't imagine these houses going for less than half a mil, at least."

Josh studied the area with a practiced eye. "They have neighborhood watch signs on most of the houses. I see a few cameras facing the roads and driveways, too."

"He's been gone for seven months. I doubt anyone has any footage from that far back," Tristan replied as he walked up the path to the front door. "And Mr. Lopez went on a business trip and never returned. There probably wouldn't be much to see, anyway."

Josh shrugged. "Weirder shit's been known to happen."

Maddox knocked on the door. Within moments, the door was opened and a smiling woman stood there until she registered who they were and then her smile slowly melted off her face. "Is it Raul? Have you found him?"

"No ma'am," Maddox was quick to correct her. "We're with the Paranormal Investigative Services. I'm Senior Special Agent Maddox Smith. These are my partners, Special Agent Tristan James and Officer Josh Bradley."

"Yes, I'm sorry. I forgot for a moment that we'd set up a meeting for today. It's been a hectic few days, and it just slipped my mind. Please come in. Can I offer you a glass of water or coffee, or I have some iced tea if you'd prefer that?"

"Water would be great." The Florida humidity was quick to make them pour sweat.

They waited for the wife to return as they scanned the room. There were pictures on the walls of the couple on various vacations. They looked happy and in love. Tristan had been a cop long enough though, to know pictures didn't always tell the truth.

"So Mrs. Lopez-"

"Please, call me Sandy," she interjected as she handed them each a bottle of water.

"Sandy, we understand your husband was away on a business trip. He checked in with you a couple of times, but when it came time to come home, he never boarded the plane in Dallas?"

"Yes, that's correct. He checked into the hotel. He attended the first day and then that was it. He called me when he'd arrived and then at the end of the night to tell me how it'd gone. The next morning, I texted him with a question about our car insurance. I needed the login for our policy. He called and walked me through it, and then said he had to go so he wasn't late. That was the last time I talked to him."

"We saw the video of him checking in and walking in the lobby on that first day." Maddox agreed. "The reports from the original investigating officers were very thorough, but they had no leads, correct?"

Sandy nodded. "I've spent the last few months talking to all his friends and coworkers. I've posted on my Facebook and his, pleading for information without any success. He hasn't touched our bank accounts, our credit cards, or anything else. It's like he just disappeared off the face of the earth." She paused as she tried not to cry, "The not knowing is the hardest part, you know."

"Mrs. Lopez," Tristan leaned forward to capture her attention, "Was he acting strange or out of character before he left? Any unusual phone calls or have you thought of anything that stands out that you didn't think about at the time, but since has made you wonder?"

Sandy frowned and shook her head. "No, nothing, and I've replayed that day over and over in my head a thousand times." She stood up and gestured for them to follow her down the hall. "This is our room," she moved to the dresser and pointed, "He left his favorite watch, the one his grandfather gave him when he was a teenager." She spun and raced over to the closet and pulled out a t-shirt on a hanger. "This shirt is priceless to him. He has it laundered to make sure it's taken care of. It's a twenty-five dollar concert shirt. It's his good luck charm."

Tristan frowned as he watched her frantic movements. He wasn't sure what the purpose of her showing them all of this was, but it was important to her, so he'd listen and pay attention.

"You have to understand, we have a good life, we were happy. Something had to have happened to him. We were planning our twentieth wedding anniversary trip for next month. It was a trip we'd talked about taking since the day we'd met. He'd be here if he could."

Tristan hated to hear the pain in her voice, statistics weren't in her favor on this one. The chances of her husband coming home were slim, but there was no way he was going to tell her that until they had no choice. Hope was a precious thing he refused to take away from anyone.

CHAPTER
Seven

MADDOX WAS BONE TIRED. All the drama between humans and supes was getting out of control. He was looking forward to a nice, relaxing family dinner.

He knocked and entered his mom's house. Tallie and Quinn were constantly giving him crap about waiting for someone to answer the door to his childhood home. They insisted he 'grow a pair' and walk in. Tallie was hard enough to deal with. Add Quinn to the mix and those two were a force to be reckoned with. He'd never been afraid of teen girls before, but those two changed all that.

He felt the tension radiating from the living room before he even stepped into the room. He glanced at Tristan, who shrugged and kept walking.

His father was sitting in the recliner with his arms folded and a glare on his too-beautiful face. Mom was across from him, staring daggers. Tallie and Quinn sat on the couch between them, looking seriously uncomfortable.

If he could have, he would have backed away and run. "Hey everyone. What's going on?"

All at once, they started talking and waving their hands around.

Tristan covered his mouth with his hand to hide his smile. He wasn't going to be much help.

Maddox whistled loudly. "One at a time. Mom, you first."

Marta sighed dramatically. "We're having a dispute over the guest list and location of the wedding."

Silas jumped in. "She's being narrow-minded. She doesn't want anyone from my side unless they are immediate family."

Maddox rolled his eyes. He wasn't surprised this argument had finally come up. "Mom. I've come to terms with both sides of who I am. You don't need to hold a grudge for me."

Tears welled in her eyes. "I didn't know how unhappy you had been with the fae. They never treated you right. So why should we invite them?"

He walked over and sat on the coffee table so he could hold her hands. "I'm sorry I made you think you needed to not like them on my behalf. I've been looking back at my childhood and you all may have been right that a lot of my isolation may have been my own fault." Tallie snorted and shook her head at him. He ignored her snark. "The fae hadn't treated me poorly, and I pushed away my ogre friends. I was a stupid kid having an identity crisis."

She pulled one of her hands free and cupped his cheek. "My poor boy. I had no idea the struggle you were having. You hid so much of it from me."

Silas had silently walked up and set his hand on Maddox's shoulder. "And I should have done more to make you feel like you belonged." He went down on one knee to look into Marta's eyes. "What better way to show everyone that we are okay with who we are and who we love than to invite them to the wedding? My family truly has always liked you. They will be thrilled to be included."

Marta looked back and forth between them. "Maddox, if you truly have no ill will toward the fae, then I will allow them. It would be nice though, if you mended some bridges with your ogre friends. A lot of them ask about you all the time." She brushed tears from her cheeks. "This can be more than just a wedding. It can be a chance for all of us to show we accept all kinds and want to bring the communities together."

Quinn chuckled. "I think they might get that just by seeing your wedding party. You have a human turned phoenix, a teenage sprite, and me... I don't know what to call whatever the heck I am, but I'll come up with something before the wedding."

The tension was instantly dispelled as everyone laughed at the truth of her statement. They really were a motley crew.

Maddox hopped up. "Now that we've settled that, can we eat?"

All four heads shook no.

Quinn held up a notebook. "We're trying to pick the dates for the bachelorette party, bachelor party, and bridal shower. Plus, we need to meet with the florist and plan the rehearsal dinner."

"I'm sorry, dear," Marta interjected. "I haven't even started cooking because we've been arguing over all this."

Tristan groaned. "I can't wait. Can we order in?"

All at once, everyone tossed out ideas of where to eat. He held his hands up. "Nope. Too many opinions. I'll pick the place, pass around my phone, and you'll put your order in."

Everyone grudgingly agreed. Silas got up from his kneeling position and patted Maddox's shoulder. "You might want to get more comfortable. Those two are planning everything and that's just one notebook of questions and to-do's."

Maddox groaned as Tallie and Quinn gave him gleeful smiles. At least they were enjoying themselves. The wedding really was the perfect distraction for Quinn, who was still only six months post-Frankenstein as he called it. He didn't think he'd be coping as well if he had been in her shoes.

Quinn flipped through the pages of her notebook and cleared her throat. "So for the bachelor party, are you thinking strip club or hiring strippers to come to you?"

All three men gave her looks of disgust.

"That's a little sexist of you to assume that Silas wants that. Not all men, straight or gay, are into that." Maddox said.

Silas nodded. "I totally agree. I want nothing to do with that. Honestly, a night out with you guys at a nice restaurant, a bottle of wine, maybe play some billiards, and I'll be a happy groom."

Tristan and Maddox let out audible sighs of relief.

"We can definitely work with that," Tristan added.

Tallie and Quinn rolled their eyes at them.

Quinn turned to Marta. "If you want, we can wait until we're alone to discuss the bachelorette party and the bridal shower. We don't need any prudish men interjecting."

Maddox put his order in the food delivery app and handed it back to Tristan. "All set. The sooner the food gets here, the sooner we can escape those two."

Tristan nodded quickly. "I'll pay the extra fee for rush delivery."

"Sometimes you guys can be mean brothers." Tallie scowled at them.

Maddox's heart melted. It was the first time she called him her brother. The little sprite was worming her way into his heart and he was so grateful he'd helped her that first day he met her rather than toss her in juvie like he was supposed to do.

Tristan reached over and absently rubbed his back. Maddox couldn't help smiling. Life really was perfect.

CHAPTER
Eight

TRISTAN TOOK a large gulp of coffee and turned to plop down into the office chair.

"Don't get comfortable. Everybody needs to suit up in riot gear." Vic tossed out as he walked into the pod. "There's a supe activist group that has set up a peaceful protest in Al Lopez park. We're going to be there to act as crowd control and to keep any troublemakers from either side out of the way so they don't escalate anything."

The team rushed to the closet and passed out P.I.S. vests and helmets to everyone. They rarely carried weapons because of their natural strength, but riots were a different story.

Once they were geared up, they met back around the pod. Vic was in full gear himself. "Use your lights. Make sure your identification is clear. I expect some human groups to try to keep us from getting to the park. Do everything you can to peacefully get there. If you can't make it in your car, go on foot or fly. Never go anywhere alone. Let's all hope this stays the peaceful protest they are advertising it as."

They bumped fists as they left. Maddox had a bad feeling about it, but he couldn't keep them from doing their jobs.

They took Tristan's truck and plugged in the emergency lights Maddox hated using. The closer they got to the park, the more people they saw congregating on the sidewalks. It was obvious by their signs which groups were on which sides of the debate.

Tristan must have known a back way because he got them there without incident. They locked up the truck and joined in with the supernatural crowd. Vic was standing under a tent with the P.I.S. logo on it. He had a map of the park laid out on a table. "I'm going to assign everyone areas to monitor. Report in if you see anything suspicious and, for god's sake, don't take out your earpieces."

They nodded and waited for him to point to where he wanted Tristan, Josh, and Maddox to patrol.

Sweat was already rolling down Tristan's back. Heat always brought out the worst in people. For the first hour, everything was calm. Supes gathered around a makeshift stage and waved their signs.

A woman eventually walked onto the stage and quieted the crowd down. "It's great to see so many of you here today. If you're here, you've seen our guest speaker on various news broadcasts and his social media channels. Jasper Pollen has always been a vocal supporter of supernatural rights. He believes in a world where we can live as equals, with no hatred between our kinds. Without further ado, please help me welcome Jasper to the stage."

The roar of the crowd was deafening as the middle-aged, raven-haired man stepped on stage. He waved at the crowd like a politician running for office. It took a full five minutes to quiet everyone down enough for him to speak.

"It brings me no joy to be standing before you today. We are facing our greatest threat since the convergence. This politician wants to tag us like animals and keep tabs on our every movement. They don't think of us as people just like they are. We are beneath them. We are unworthy of having the same rights as them. And I'm here to say we will not stand for it."

The crowd screamed loudly. Chants of his name rolled across the park.

The familiar sound of helicopter blades overtook the noise from the people. It flew low over them as paper fell from its open doors.

Tristan grabbed one sheet out of the air. "Fucking Hell."

It was a flier saying supernaturals deserved to be in cages like the monsters they were. Anger rippled across the crowd as people read the flyers. Jasper held one up in the air, waiting to address the latest threat.

Ensley's voice crackled in their ears. "He's going to get shot."

No one heard the gun go off as a bullet flew across the crowd and hit its mark. Jasper didn't even have time to react. The bullet lodged in his chest and killed him instantly.

"Shit," Tristan yelled as chaos reigned as people ducked low to the ground and raced from the area, not caring who was in front of them or who they stepped on to get away. People shifted, some flew away. He raced into the fleeing crowd and helped pull people to their feet as quickly as he could. He saw his teammates doing the same. Within minutes, the park had emptied until only the Agents and a few bystanders who were hiding behind trees and bushes remained.

"Any sign of where it came from?" Vic demanded as he scanned the area. "Anyone see anything?"

A chorus of no's filled their earpieces as Tristan debated the wisdom of them being out in the open like this. Chances were the gunmen had already fled, but there was nothing saying the asshole was sane in the first place.

Sirens filled the air, alerting them that someone had called in the reinforcements and ambulances. Tristan knew it was too late for Jasper, though.

"Captain?"

Vic nodded absently as he continued surveying the scene. "We need to know where that shot came from and find out if he's still here. We can't risk the EMTs until we know the scene is secure."

Maddox moved to stand beside Vic. "With the podium, the shot would have had to come from one of those buildings. Can we send in the TPD to clear them so we can let the paramedics tend to those who were injured in the rush?"

Vic nodded. "I'll radio it in. Anyone that isn't self-healing we need to help out of the park where the EMTs are on standby. Until those buildings are cleared, I don't want anyone coming in here."

Maddox nodded and turned back to the team. "You heard him. Let's get these people to safety. Be careful. We don't know if the shooter is still out there or not."

Ensley paced, flexing her hands into fists. "I'm sorry, guys. I didn't get the vision fast enough."

Vic pulled her to a stop. "No one blames you. You only had a second's notice before the shot was fired. There is nothing else you could have done."

She nodded, but Maddox could tell she was going to beat herself up over that for a while.

Over the next two hours, the team processed all the parkgoers. It was tedious to have everyone checked out by the EMTs and document their statements. As Tristan knew would happen, no one had anything helpful to report. Everyone had been watching the speech, not the building behind them.

By the time they were clear to leave the scene to the forensic teams, they were exhausted mentally and physically. All Tristan wanted to do was take a long, hot shower and wash away the ugliness of the day.

As they headed back to the truck, Tristan sighed. "We missed the interview we had set up."

"I called and rescheduled. She was watching the news and saw the speech. She was fine with rescheduling till later in the week." Josh explained as he opened the back door and climbed in. "I can honestly say I didn't expect this task force to be quite like this."

Tristan nodded emphatically. "No shit, I say that every day on this job, though. I honestly never know what each day is going to bring."

Maddox snorted. "You know, before you came along, things were pretty chill. Sure, we had crime, but it sure seems like shit's gotten crazy since you turned." Maddox reached across and rested his hand on Tristan's thigh. "And I wouldn't have it any other way."

"If you two are done being lovey-dovey and shit, I'd love to get this gear off and head home to my wife. She's been blowing up my phone for the last few hours and she isn't going to stop until she sees me for herself and knows I'm okay."

Tristan laughed as he put the truck into gear and headed off. "As much as I used to complain about the people in my life being needy and demanding answers about things. It was nice to know they cared too. Let's get you home, so I can go home and hold my man and know he's safe too."

CHAPTER
Nine

MADDOX STRETCHED as he got out of the truck. It had been a hell of a day and he was ready to go home and pretend none of it had happened.

On their way into the office, a woman came around the corner and stepped right in front of them. "Please. You have to help me."

Maddox looked around for someone chasing her. "What's wrong, ma'am?"

"They've taken my family, and I don't know how to get any answers about them. I don't know where they took them or if they're okay."

"Who took your family?" Tristan asked.

"I don't know. They looked like soldiers." Tears poured down her face.

Maddox blew out a breath. His night wasn't

ending anytime soon. "How about we go inside and you can explain it from the start?"

Josh held the door open and let them lead her to the conference room on their floor. Tristan grabbed their riot gear and went to put it away while Maddox got her situated and gave her a cup of coffee.

Tristan returned with a laptop and a notepad.

Maddox waited until Josh was seated before starting.

"Let's start with your name."

"Ceka Tora. My husband's name is Ikina and my children are Kumiko, Sora, and Keiko."

Tristan typed the names into the computer. No record of them came up in the shifter database or any other law enforcement system. He tilted the screen so Maddox could see the results.

Not showing up in the shifter database wasn't possible. Something wasn't adding up. "Ma'am, we have no record of any of you."

She nodded. "Of course you wouldn't. We had only come through the rift minutes before the soldiers came and grabbed us. I got away, but they rounded up everyone that had come through with us."

Maddox glanced at Tristan and Josh, who looked

just as lost. "What do you mean, you came through a rift?"

It was her turn to look confused. "The rifts... the tears that keep opening up between this realm and the paranormal realm. They started showing up a few years ago but were never open long enough for anyone to get through. We hadn't found a way to track when they would open, so when one did, you were packed and ready to leave at a moment's notice. It was only recently that they started staying open for a few minutes at a time."

Maddox covered his mouth and blew out a breath. What in the hell was she talking about?

Tristan shook his head as if to clear it, "Are you saying that rifts, like the one that caused our worlds to collide in the first place? Scientists closed that and we've not had anything like that happen since... right?"

Maddox nodded. "It's been decades since that happened and there has never been any mention of rifts opening. Not that we don't believe you. You just threw a curveball at us."

"I wasn't the greatest of students in school, but didn't they teach us that the other side, the paranormal realm, was decimated in the fusion? But you're telling us you're from there and there are others as well?"

She nodded eagerly. "I don't know what they've told you, but when they closed it, there were many of us still trapped on the other side. We learned to survive, but it's not easy. There is nothing left. We all dreamed of coming here and reuniting with those on this side one day."

Josh cursed as he shook his head. "I'm really struggling with this knowledge. I probably shouldn't be. Our government has a known history of doing shady shit to our own people. So why should I expect anything different when they're dealing with those they thought of as different?"

"Do you have somewhere safe to hide right now?" Maddox asked.

She nodded. "There's a network here of others who have also crossed. They help hide new arrivals and get us acclimated to this world. They said the government has been getting faster and faster at detecting the rifts and catching people as soon as they crossed. I was under the impression they've taken thousands over the last couple of years." She pointed at the pen and paper in Tristan's hand. He slid the notepad across the table. "This is the number of the device they gave me for emergencies.

I'm not far from here. I can't give up on my family. They're all I have."

Maddox nodded. "I understand. Let us look into this a little more. If you hear anything else that may be useful, please let us know." He handed her his card. "We'll be in touch soon."

Josh stood up and held the door open. "I'll walk her out. I'll see you guys in the morning."

Once they were alone, Maddox turned to Tristan. "What the fuck? Rifts? Supes are still alive on that side? Secret prisoners? I'm struggling here. I know we've had a seriously shit day, but I can't fathom any of this is true."

Tristan gathered up the notepad and computer. "There's nothing else we can do tonight and the whole team has had a bad day. Why don't we go home, reset, and we'll catch everyone up in the morning?"

That sounded perfect to Maddox. He needed a few hours of quiet and peacefulness holding Tristan in his arms. The rest of the bullshit could wait until tomorrow.

CHAPTER

Ten

TRISTAN LAID his head down on the table in the pod and sighed. "When did things get so complicated? How are we even supposed to explain this and not sound insane? I mean, I was there and I question if it really happened."

"No shit." Josh agreed as he walked in with a large cup of coffee. "I've been trying to wrap my head around this, and I can't. I drove my wife crazy with my pacing and mutterings all night. I thought about searching on my home computer, but then thought twice about that. Am I being paranoid?"

Vic walked in and whistled. "I think this is the first time you guys have ever been the first ones here."

Maddox grimaced. "It's not for good reasons. We have a lot to talk about once everyone has arrived."

"Why do I suddenly feel the need for antacids?" Vic muttered as he studied each of their faces in turn.

"Get me some while you're at it," Josh tossed out as he continued to pace the pod.

Time ticked slowly as everyone came in. The air in the room must have been charged, since their smiles faded as soon as they saw them.

"Okay. We have a shit ton to talk about with yesterday's debacle, but we need to hear out Maddox and team. Guys go ahead."

"When we got back last night, there was a woman waiting for us. She was begging for help to find her family." Tristan frowned as he thought back to the night before. "Maybe her appearance should have been the first indicator something was off." He said absently, before shaking his head and looking around at the group. "She said they came through a rift that had opened from the paranormal realm. Her family had been captured by soldiers, but she'd escaped."

"She claims there are still people on the other side, in our old realm. She said the rifts started opening a few years ago and lately have been open for longer and longer periods. They are struggling to survive on that side, so they all want to cross. There is a network here that helps these people. They say the government has been getting quicker at finding the rifts and has secretly imprisoned thousands."

Gasps went around the room.

"Cole, do you think you can do your computer mojo shit and see if you can find any chatter about this? Search the dark web or wherever it is you find out shit that no one else can," Tristan asked after the lull had gone on for a few minutes.

Cole nodded as he opened his laptop. "I haven't heard anything about rifts, but if you give me a minute, I'll let you know for sure. If it's out there, I'll find it."

Vic stood up and sighed as he moved to grab a cup of coffee. "My antacids need a chaser." He grumbled as he popped a couple of the pills. "While he's researching, let's talk about last night and where everything stands."

"I still can't believe that happened. I mean, we were there to do crowd control, but I don't think any of us really believed there would be an assassination. It took quite a few stiff drinks for me to get to sleep last night." Raelle said as she rubbed her temples.

Murmurs of agreement echoed around the room.

"I had dreams all night of the faces of the group of teens that were near me. They were sure they were going to die. And for a few minutes, I wasn't sure if I was going to be able to save them if it had gotten worse. We really lucked out that the person who did this only went after the speaker. Can you imagine if they had just started firing into the crowd, too?" Sheppard added.

Vic went back to the table and sat down with a weary huff. "TPD found the room where the shooter had been hiding, but the person got away. Their forensics is leading the investigation, but we've assigned our own forensics team to work hand in hand with them. We're planning to strong-arm them into letting us run most of the tests since our systems are better than theirs, but we're having a pissing contest over it right now." He rolled his eyes. "We'll also be working on the case from our side. Jasmina, Kiely, and Lexi have closed three of their missing persons cases, so they are going to take the lead on the assassination."

Maddox's jaw dropped. "You closed three cases in three days?"

Kiely smiled proudly. "One was alive and well. The second was murdered by a jealous husband, and the third was addicted to that super meth for supes and was out on the streets. We're still working the other two cases."

"If one was murdered, why was it still listed as a missing person?" Tristan grumbled. "Were they given the easy cases or something?"

Vic rolled his eyes in exasperation as Jasmina stuck out her tongue at him. "It's called being a good agent. You should try it sometime."

Tristan laughed, but before he could retort, Vic interrupted. "The TPD closed that case, but failed to update the case because of some computer glitch, or at least that's what they reported when I questioned them about it."

Cole slammed on his keyboard repeatedly. "No, no, no," He growled as he pushed his laptop away. "Someone just got into my system and booted me."

Every phone in the room pinged at the same time.

Tristan grabbed his phone from his pants pocket and scowled as he read the message. "Did we all get the same message?"

"This is your first and only warning. Stop looking into things that are of no concern to you." Jaylen read out loud. "That message?"

"Fuck me," Maddox grumbled. "That's some secret spy shit right there."

"Hey Cole," Tristan turned to face the other man, "Don't take this the wrong way, but I thought you were like the best of the best. How the hell did they get into your computer and kick you out?"

Cole blew out a breath. "I'm good, damn good, but I wouldn't say the best. But that being said, there is no fucking way they should have been able to get through my security like that."

"You know what freaks me out, besides the fact they know what we were talking about and messaged all of us at once," Raelle said as she scanned each of their faces. "Is that my phone was on silent and they turned the sound on. That's just fucked up."

"Right! How did they know who was in the room?" Willow said as she chewed her nail nervously.

Derek nodded. "I suddenly feel way over my head with all of this."

Vic scribbled on a notepad as he walked toward the corner of the room. "Everyone stop and take a breath. We are a government agency. This isn't a movie. No one is going to come kill us in our sleep. I'll work with Cole and our cyber division on this, and you all get back to your cases." He held up the notepad with the words 'Turn off phones any time you discuss this and try to stay out of view of cameras.'

Tristan could feel his eyes bug out of his head at Vic's words. What in the hell had they gotten themselves into?

CHAPTER
Eleven

MADDOX DROPPED into the chair at his desk and blew out a breath. His mind was going a mile a minute. As if everything wasn't already going to hell, now they were suddenly being pulled into some conspiracy shit, too.

Josh clicked his pen repeatedly as his leg shook up and down. "I knew this task force was going to be a unique experience, but damn. Every day just seems to get crazier."

"If it makes you feel any better, we don't have anywhere to be until four o'clock, so maybe we can have a few hours of normalcy. Let's order lunch in and we can spend the day researching our vic's." Maddox pulled a file of takeout menus from his desk. "Newbies choice."

"How about Thai? My wife isn't a fan, but I love it and never get it." Josh licked his lips as he flipped through the large stack. "Do you guys have one for every restaurant within a fifty-mile radius?"

Tristan laughed. "No, just the places that will deliver to us. Though I think at least half of these menus are for places that went out of business. Maddox is cute, but he doesn't like to throw things away."

"More like I'm too lazy." Maddox tossed over his shoulder.

"And considering he has such a phobia of commitment, it makes you wonder why he held on to these..." Tristan winked at Maddox's annoyed look.

Josh scribbled something on a notepad and passed it. "Well, that's what I want. Just let me know who to send money to."

"Maddox, order my usual please," Tristan called out as he grabbed a file and opened it. "These cases haven't been touched in a bit, so I thought I'd start running them through the different databases and see if anything new pops up."

Maddox grunted his acknowledgment while he opened the delivery app and placed the order. He tossed his phone down and turned back to his computer. "And now I have to find a missing gopher. How hard can that be?"

The room went silent as everyone focused on their own cases. Once in a while, the printer would go or there would be pings when results came back from searches.

Maddox's stomach growled just as the knock came on their office door. Finneas stood there with a smile on his face and their food in his hand. "Hey, guys. Long time no see. I was in the lobby and heard your name given, so I offered to bring this up." He handed the bags to Josh. "And who is this?"

Josh set the food down and held out his hand. "I'm Josh. One of the humans who joined the task force."

Finneas' eyes lit up. "Humans... I heard you guys would be joining us." He glanced at Maddox. "You get all the fun, don't you?"

Why did everything the fae said to him sound like flirting? Maybe it was just him, but Finneas always made him feel like he was a piece of meat. He did his usual grunt and continued reading the report on his screen.

"I'm not sure fun is the right word at the moment, but it's pretty awesome to have Josh and the others here." Tristan agreed with a subtle kick to

Maddox's chair. "How are things going with you? All settled in here finally?"

Finneas nodded with a beautiful smile that lit up his face. "I am. I'm really excited I got to come work here with all of you. Everyone has been so fantastic and made me feel right at home. I couldn't ask for more. I offered to help with the shooting yesterday, so hopefully, I'll be able to spend more time up here with you."

Maddox purposely didn't look, but he swore the too-beautiful man was staring at him.

"Fuck." Everyone turned to stare at him. "Sorry, ignore me." No way was he going to admit that he had fallen back into his old ways. He'd been trying so hard to forgive the fae and be more tolerant and one look at Finneas and he forgot all of it.

Tristan gave him a questioning look. He shook his head, hoping he'd get he wanted him to leave it alone for now.

"Well anyway. You have your food and it was nice meeting you, Josh." Finneas waved at everyone and left.

Josh and Tristan turned to look at him.

"Don't worry about it. Just eat your food." That was the problem with sharing a tiny office. Everyone was in everyone else's business.

An hour later, Maddox got the hit he'd been hoping for. "You guys are going to love this. Sheila had won the state lottery four weeks before her disappearance. She'd stayed quiet, but as soon as her money came in, she fell off the grid. A little more digging into her bank statements and I'd found a lawyer who had helped her relocate to a small village in Italy."

"Do you need to set up a call with her in Italy to confirm it's her?" Josh asked.

Maddox nodded. "I'll reach out to the lawyer and ask him to pass along my info to Sheila, asking her to let us know she's okay, so we can close her case."

He got up and poked his head out the door. "Kiely," he waited for her to pop her head out of her office. "We closed one."

She rolled her eyes at him. "Good job. Two to go to catch up."

"You're on."

Vic poked his head out of his office. "You know these are people's lives, right? It's not supposed to be a competition." Laughter rang out from every office in the pod. He shook his head. "And these are the agents I get stuck with."

"You love us, you know it." Maddox shot back before going back to his desk.

"I have to wonder if you guys were always like this, or if somehow there's been an influence that has inspired such childish antics." Josh gave Maddox a pointed look.

Maddox mock gasped. "Childish? Being competitive is a good thing. It keeps us sharp and eager. We have one of the best close records in the whole building."

Tristan fake coughed, "Humble brag."

Maddox shrugged as he crossed Sheila's name off the whiteboard. "If you got it, flaunt it."

"That's what he said." Tristan grinned as he turned back to his computer. "Or should I say, that's what you said last night, too?"

"No." Josh groaned as he stood up. "We've got to go soon to make the interview we rescheduled, or did you forget about that?"

"A good agent would never forget. Let's go."

The trio hopped into Tristan's truck and drove to the University of Tampa. This was always one of his favorite buildings to drive by. It looked like it was transported from Russia to the heart of Tampa, onion domes, and all.

Tristan pulled into the campus police station and waited while Maddox ran in. The human officer at the counter wasn't outright nasty, but he wasn't happy to see him, either. He gave him a parking pass with a map to the library.

He hung the tag on the rearview mirror and handed the map to Tristan.

It was a five-minute drive and lucky for them, their pass let them park in the law enforcement spot.

Josh pointed at a girl standing under a tree. "That's her."

The trio walked up and held up their badges. "Ms Danson? I'm Senior Special Agent Maddox Smith and these are my partners, Special Agent Tristan James and Officer Josh Bradley. Is there somewhere we can talk more privately?"

"I booked a study room for an hour." She pointed at the library behind her.

They followed her inside. They had gotten used to the people staring at them. They probably should have offered to walk a bit behind her, so it didn't look like they were escorting or protecting her.

She pointed to a hallway on the left. "The supe rooms are this way."

Maddox looked right and saw the sign for 'Human Only Study Rooms'. "Do you guys have separate books, too?"

"No. I think they realize that wouldn't be very cost-effective. We do have separate check-out areas, so for the most part it's no big deal." She shrugged as she opened the door to the tiny room and let them enter first.

Once they were settled, Tristan pulled out his notepad.

"Why don't you tell us about the days leading up to Maria's disappearance? Did you notice anything unusual? Was she acting out of character? Or mention being followed?"

The poor girl's knee bounced up and down under the table. "Everything was cool. She was doing good in her classes. She'd been on a couple of dates, but nothing serious. She was saving up money to fly home to Denver for the holidays, so she did a lot of babysitting jobs. That night, she was going to a new client's house. She'd talked with the couple a few times and got pictures of the kids. She left just before dinner and promised to message me when she got there. She never did and her location stopped sharing in the neighborhood where she was supposed to be babysitting. Your agents later told me that the family didn't exist." She ended with a shud-dered breath.

Maddox gave the girl credit. She was holding it together. Barely, but that counted.

"The school let us set up search parties, and we

collected money for a reward, but she literally just disappeared into thin air."

"We're waiting for a call back from her family. Do you still have contact with them?" Maddox asked.

"I check in with them weekly. It's always the same. None of us have heard anything."

This time, the tears rolled down her face. Josh handed her a tissue he'd pulled from a pouch in his pocket.

Maddox lifted an eyebrow at him. He shrugged. Maddox slid his card across the table. "If you think of anything else, don't hesitate to reach out."

She nodded and cried harder. All three men looked at each other.

"We'll let you go now. Have a good night." Maddox said quickly before escaping the room.

When they got back to the car, everyone let out a heavy breath.

"Why do I feel like we're wasting our time with these interviews?" Tristan asked as he looked back at the campus. "Have we learned anything of use at all?"

Josh shrugged. "I've learned a ton, but that's because I've never been on a paranormal case before."

"Okay, but I was more talking about learning

something about the missing people, but I'm glad you're getting something out of this, I guess." Tristan rolled his eyes with a small laugh. "Guess you can teach an old dog new tricks."

Maddox scrolled through his messages on his phone as Tristan pulled out of the parking lot. "Unfortunately, we have to do these interviews. We all know anything we find is going to be through research or boots on the ground."

"Can we at least have Antonio's agent come to the office for his interview?" Tristan asked as he merged into traffic. "He was supposed to call and tell us when we could meet him tomorrow."

"If he's willing to come in, I'm good with it," Maddox answered without looking up from his phone.

"Hey Maddox," Josh interrupted the silence a few minutes later. "Any chance once we close this case you'll take me for a spin in Scarlet? I feel like it's a rite of passage and I'm being left out."

"I'm always happy to take Scarlet out for a drive. We just need to get rid of this guy for a bit." he pointed at Tristan. "Unless he wants to fold up into a tiny ball in the backseat. Which could be kind of fun if I take the corners hard enough."

"I'm seriously not feeling the love here." Tristan shot back.

Maddox reached over and squeezed his thigh. "I'm sorry, babe. I'll make it up to you later, promise."

CHAPTER
Twelve

TRISTAN HIT submit on his report and sat back in his chair with a sigh. Now that he'd written up his observations of the interview, he was finally free for the day. He couldn't wait to go home, pop open a cold beer, and relax with Maddox.

"You done finally?" Josh asked as he turned off his computer. "I swear you type slower than my grandmother and she doesn't know how to use a computer."

Tristan flicked him off. "Maybe I'm just more observant and therefore had more to say."

Josh laughed, said good night, and headed out the door. Maddox watched him go with a smile and then turned back to Tristan, "Come on, I've got something to show you."

"Babe, I thought Vic told you no sexy times at work," Tristan smirked as he followed out of the office. "Not that I'm opposed to the idea, mind you. I'll just tell him you compromised me if we get caught."

Maddox didn't reply, just kept walking, which made Tristan even more curious. Was there something in this building he hadn't seen at this point? He should get brownie points for blindly following his lover without too much complaining.

"I knew it." Tristan exclaimed as Maddox led him into the locker rooms, "I'm so sexy you can't wait to get me home, can you?"

"Keep it in your pants. I'm not always trying to have sex." Maddox threw over his shoulder.

"Well, what are we doing in here, then?" Tristan asked as he looked around, perplexed. "I've been in here before, so what could you possibly have to show me if it's not you naked?"

Maddox rolled his eyes. "Do you trust me?"

"Of course."

"Good, then shut up, close your eyes, and don't open them until I say so." Maddox waited until Tristan obeyed him and then grabbed his hand. "Okay, I'm going to lead you out now."

"If this is a trap, I will make you pay later," Tristan warned as he listened intently, trying to figure out what was happening and where he was being led to. He felt the air shift as they went through a door.

"All set?" Maddox asked as he pulled Tristan to a stop just inside the gym.

"Yup, to your exact specifications." Logan agreed.

"Hi, Logan," Tristan called out. "Fancy meeting you here."

"Tristan, I'm going to let go of you, but don't open your eyes until I say so. Deal?"

Tristan scowled, but nodded. "It's not like I haven't seen the gym before. What's with all the secrecy?"

He felt Maddox move behind him as he listened for some sign of what was happening around him. Just when he thought he'd go crazy in anticipation, Maddox told him he could open his eyes.

"Woah," Tristan exclaimed in surprise as he took in the made-over gym. "What is all this?"

"You remember when we went to the school, and they had that room for the kids to practice flying? Well, I thought since we've been so busy with everything happening, that maybe you'd like to try it.

Then I thought you wouldn't want to do it in front of the kids, so I enlisted Logan to help create something similar here for you to use."

"You guys did this for me?" Tristan couldn't believe his eyes. Everywhere he looked, he saw platforms of varying heights. Padded mats covered the ground to provide a soft landing place. "I'm not sure if I'm more excited or scared to try this. Hell, I'm even a bit turned on that you thought to do this. It's amazing." He turned and grabbed Maddox by the cheeks, "You are the best boyfriend a guy could have. Thank you for doing this for me." He kissed him and then turned to Logan. "Thank you, Logan. This is beyond awesome."

"Just don't kiss me and we'll call it even." Logan winked.

Tristan laughed as he turned around to face the gym again. "Okay, so what do I need to know to do this? I mean, how do you learn to fly? Do I just jump and hope my wings will hold me up?"

"Well, if you need help getting your wings out, I'm happy to help with that. You know I love slapping your ass." Maddox winked at him. "Seriously though, you understand gravity and lift and drag. It's all the same. Plus, I'll be there to slow your descent if you do start to plummet and the mats should cushion you some."

"I could be at the bottom waiting to catch you, but that just sounds painful. You're a big boy. I'm sure you'll bounce off the ground just fine." Logan added with a shit-eating grin.

"Wow, I'm totally feeling the love here," Tristan called as he stopped under the first platform. "I'm really debating if I should start at a small one or go for the tallest, so I have more time to figure it out before I could possibly hit the ground."

He looked from spot to spot before finally shrugging and climbing the one he was standing in front of. It wasn't the tallest, but it was close. And he knew if he waited too long to decide, he'd probably figure out a reason not to do it.

"Okay, so I just jump off and hope my wings know what to do?" Tristan asked as he climbed up on top and peered over the edge.

"You might want to have your wings pop out before you jump, just in case," Logan called out helpfully. "I mean, I don't have wings and I've never flown, but it seems logical at least."

Tristan grunted as he shot Logan a dirty look. "Thanks, captain obvious."

He blew out a breath and focused on bringing his wings out. He loved the feeling of having them free like this.

Maddox stepped up next to him and released his wings. "Just follow me." He bent his knees slightly and dove like he would into a swimming pool. He fell for a few feet before his wings caught the current and lifted him. He circled around the roof. A few times, he dipped near Tristan and then back up again. "Okay, babe. Your turn."

"Did you have to consciously tell your wings to flap, or they just did it?" Tristan asked as he stepped closer to the edge and looked down once more.

"Stop overthinking it and just jump. Your body knows what to do." Maddox yelled down from above.

"Easy for you to say. You were born with your wings," Tristan grumbled as he closed his eyes and took a deep breath. "This better work, or you're sleeping on the couch for a week." He yelled as he stepped over the edge.

He wanted to scream, but his asshole was in his throat blocking all sound from escaping as he felt the air rush past him. Just when he thought for sure he was going to hit the ground, his wings started to flap and he hovered inches from the mats.

"Well, you stopped yourself. That's a good start, right?" Logan offered with a grimace.

Maddox landed beside him and smiled. "That wasn't so bad, was it?"

Tristan scowled, "Fuck off. If you tell anyone how bad that went, I will make you both pay."

He could hear their snickering as he climbed back up the ladder and to the edge. He was determined this time to fly at least a little bit. If the kids could do it, he could. No way was he going to let a bunch of kids in single digits show him up.

"You got this, babe." Maddox hollered encouragingly from the ground.

"No, I don't." He mumbled as he readied himself to jump once again. "Don't think just let your body do its thing. Your wings know what to do. Trust them." He was losing his mind, he was sure of it. Why else would he be talking out loud, giving himself a fucking pep talk?

"One... two... three..." He yelled out and then jumped as he said the last number. This time he did his best to clear his mind of everything and just feel the breeze whip by him. He could feel his wings flapping for all they were worth, but the closer to the ground he got, the more worried he became. Maybe his wings weren't strong enough to hold him up long enough to fly.

As he landed on the hard ground, he let out a pained moan. "Maybe I'm not cut out for this."

Maddox squatted beside him and shook his head, "Maybe you're just overthinking the whole thing."

"We could always go to the roof and try that. Maybe he just needs a little more height and the knowledge that the ground isn't padded." Logan offered.

"He's trying to kill me, baby," Tristan whined.

"Bears are all about tough love. You don't want to know how rough we have it as cubs." He gave them a haunted look.

Maddox held out his hand to help Tristan off the floor. "I have an idea. Come on up with me, and let's try something."

Tristan groaned as he climbed to his feet and followed Maddox up the ladder. "Just to clarify, you can't take out life insurance on me without being married, right? This isn't your way of killing me off…"

Maddox laughed as he moved to the side to let Tristan stand beside him. "I think we need to get you out of your head while we do this. So, we're going to jump together. I can fly, and I'll pull you with me until your wings start working properly."

"Or you just want me to fall from a higher spot so it hurts more when I land." Tristan shook his head as he grabbed Maddox's offered hand, "It's a damn good thing I trust your ass."

Before he could think twice about it, Maddox leaped over the side, dragging Tristan with him. He could feel his wings battering the air, as Maddox did his best to hold them both aloft.

"Relax and let your body do its job. You're fighting it." Maddox gritted out between clenched teeth. "Imagine how the wind will feel against your wings as you glide through the currents."

Tristan closed his eyes and did his best to picture the words. He could hear the whoosh of the air as it rushed by his head, and could feel his feathers fluttering in the breeze.

"That's it, babe, you're doing it," Maddox called out with a laugh. "Open your eyes and look, you're flying."

"Holy shit." Tristan laughed as he flew around the gym. He never imagined it would be like this. He felt free and light and so freaking happy.

"You ready to land and go home and celebrate?" Maddox asked as he flew a circle around Tristan.

"Land?" He repeated stupidly. They hadn't discussed landing. How the hell was he supposed to do that? Was he just supposed to stop and crash? Why didn't they explain any of this before they had him flying thirty feet in the air?

CHAPTER
Thirteen

"BABE, you're a shifter. Stop being so dramatic. The pain will go away before you know it. It's probably already gone and you're just milking this for all it's worth." Maddox said as he opened the front door and led Tristan inside.

"Not true. I hit the ground hard... a couple of times." Tristan shot back as he headed to their room.

Maddox rolled his eyes as he followed his boyfriend. He loved the pain in the ass, even at times like this. "Why don't you get cleaned up? I'll make us a quick sandwich, and then I'll give you a massage."

Tristan beamed at Maddox. "Even though I'm complaining right now, I really loved what you did for me tonight. It was amazing and fun and scary as shit. Thank you for doing it."

"It was my pleasure." Maddox pulled Tristan into a hug. "Now, go clean up, and let me take care of my man."

He waited for Tristan to go into the bathroom before turning and heading back to the kitchen. They'd used a lot of energy flying tonight and for someone like Tristan, who wasn't used to it, it would hit him hard. He made quick work of putting together a couple of ham, turkey, and roast beef sandwiches with copious amounts of cheese. His man needed sustenance to replenish himself.

"I come bearing gifts," Maddox called as he entered the bedroom again and found Tristan sitting on the edge of the bed in all his naked glory. "Eat. It'll help you feel better."

"Thanks." Tristan smiled as he grabbed one of the thick sandwiches and took a huge bite. "Why does this taste so freaking good?"

Maddox laughed as he sat beside him and ate his. They lapsed into silence as they finished their meal. He took the now empty plate and placed it on the nightstand. "Lay down on the bed on your stomach and let me ease some of those sore muscles of yours."

Tristan obeyed without question, which always turned Maddox on. He loved seeing that side of his lover. He smiled as he walked into the bathroom and gathered the lotion and lube. Chances were he'd be inside him before the night was over and he didn't want to stop the momentum once it got going.

"Babe, you didn't fall asleep on me, did you?"

Tristan laughed, "Fuck no, I know you're getting ready to have your hands all over me. No way am I ever going to miss a second of that."

Maddox smiled as he stripped down and climbed on the bed so he was straddling Tristan's ass. He poured some lotion into his hands and rubbed them together to try and heat it up a bit.

"Mmmm," Tristan moaned as Maddox rubbed his shoulders and down his back. "Feels so good. Your hands are amazing."

Maddox laughed, "So I've been told."

Tristan cocked one eye open and glared over his shoulder at him. "Not really the time to boast about your past conquests."

"Don't assume that's what I meant." Maddox grinned as he hit a tender spot that made Tristan moan louder. "You're so tight."

"That's what he said." Tristan giggled.

Maddox shook his head with a smile. "I think that's what I said last night, too." He moved his hands down to Tristan's lower back and pushed on the muscles there.

"You go a little lower and you can find out for sure just how tight I am."

"Oh, I plan to. First, I need to make sure all your sore muscles are loose. Can't have you locking up while I'm pounding into your sweet ass, I'd never hear the end of it. And knowing you, you'd tell the whole office it was my fault when you call out sick tomorrow."

Tristan laughed because he knew he was right. "Damn right, I would. It's a badge of honor, though. How many guys can say they fucked their man so good, he hurt himself?"

It took all Maddox had not to rut against Tristan's ass. The friction from leaning forward and backward to reach his back was driving him insane. Add all the little moans and gasps of pleasure and he was rock fucking hard. Maddox licked his lips as he shifted backward onto Tristan's thighs.

"Babe, please touch me."

"I am." Maddox grinned as he grabbed Tristan's ass cheeks in his hands and gave them a squeeze. He grabbed the bottle of lube and quickly poured a liberal amount onto his cock and his fingers. Then he spread Tristan open and let the cold liquid dribble down his crack.

"Fuck, a little warning would have gone a long way," Tristan grumbled.

Maddox laughed, "Lube incoming, then my fingers, and finally my cock. Is that enough warning for you?"

"Ass."

It was taking all he had not to plow into Tristan and fuck him until the neighbors heard his cries of ecstasy. He didn't think he'd ever get enough of this man in his bed, his arms, or his life.

He pressed one finger against Tristan's hole and tapped, letting him know what was coming.

"Stop playing around. I need you in me," Tristan demanded.

"As you wish." Maddox pushed in through the tight ring and moaned at the sensation. "I love how hot you are for me already."

Tristan moaned and tried to shift and force him in deeper. "More, please. I need more."

Maddox pulled out and then inserted two fingers and pumped a few times until the fit wasn't quite so tight, then added a third. It only took minutes for Tristan to start to whimper and beg again. "You think you're ready for my cock? It's going to be a tight fit like this. You sure you don't want me to loosen you up some more first?"

"Fuck me, damn it. I'm ready. I need you." Tristan demanded.

"What a bossy bottom you are." Maddox smacked his ass and then spread his cheeks so he could see his destination clearly as he shifted so his cock rubbed up and down his crack. "This what you want, babe?"

"Yes, please fuck me."

He knew he'd never get tired of hearing Tristan beg him like this. It was a heady feeling, knowing he could drive this strong man to the edge so quickly. He pushed his cock through the ring of muscle and waited for him to adjust before he slowly pushed in inch by inch until his balls were pressed tight against Tristan's ass. "So fucking tight, baby. I love watching you take me like this. You were made for me, weren't you?"

"Fuck yes, for you, only you," Tristan cried out. "You feel so big like this, the stretch, the burn, move damn you. I need more."

Maddox didn't say anything this time. He couldn't because all his focus was on not coming like a teenager after his first orgasm. He pulled out and pushed in, watching as he disappeared inside his tight channel. If he could live here inside him, he would. There was no place he'd rather be. "Grab the headboard baby, I can't hold back."

"Fuck yes," Tristan cried out as he did as he was told.

He pistoned his hips, until the only sound was their grunts, moans, and the slapping of their skin. He used his left hand to hold on to Tristan's waist for leverage, and his right hand to keep him spread open so he could watch his love take him deep with each thrust.

"You going to come on my cock? Wish you could see how gorgeous you are spread open like this, your hole sucking me in and milking me. You're so hot and tight." Maddox pulled out and slapped Tristan's ass. "Up on your knees, head down."

Tristan pulled his knees under him and spread his legs so Maddox could get between them.

"Don't touch yourself until I say you can, got it?"

Tristan's only response was a whimper of need that made Maddox moan at the needy sound. He lined himself up and slammed inside. "My ass to take when I want it. You belong to me, baby."

"Yes, yours. Only yours." Tristan babbled as he fisted the sheets. "Holy fuck, yes. Like that."

"You love this, don't you? You love when I ride

your ass so hard you can't walk the next day, don't you? You love knowing how much I want you." Maddox bit out between his clenched teeth, so lost in the sensations he wasn't even fully aware of what he was saying. "I love how needy you are for my cock."

"Yes," Tristan cried out as he pushed back into the next thrust.

"Fuck, that's it." Maddox said as he felt Tristan clench around him, "You want my cum, baby. You want me to fill you up and mark you from the inside?"

"Please," Tristan begged as he tried to shift so his head wasn't hitting the headboard with each of Maddox's powerful thrusts. "I need to come. Please let me come."

Maddox grinned as he pulled out until only the tip was still inside his mate. "With me, come with me, my love." He slammed back in with a punishing rhythm that left both of them unable to speak more than a grunt or moan. He knew he wasn't going to last much longer. It felt too good to be inside Tristan. He reached around and stroked his mate's cock. That's all it took as he fell off the side of the cliff and screamed out, which made Maddox follow him. Just like in life, where one went, the other was going to follow.

Tristan collapsed onto the bed panting as he smiled softly, "Fucking hell... that was... so hot."

Maddox moaned but couldn't make himself say anything else yet. His mind was blown. Once he'd caught his breath, he pulled out of Tristan and slipped to his side so he could pull him into his arms so they were face to face.

"Hey, look at me." He stroked Tristan's cheek until he opened his eyes. "I love you, Tristan James." He had wanted to say it earlier, but didn't want him to think it was something he was saying in the heat of the moment.

Tristan's mouth dropped open in shock before he smiled and leaned in for a deep kiss. "I love you to the moon and back."

Maddox smiled as he closed his eyes and reveled in the feeling of happiness from hearing those words come from his man. A year ago, if someone had told him he'd be living with a human turned supe and telling him he loved him, he'd have laughed his ass off. Now, he couldn't imagine life any other way. Tristan was his life.

TRISTAN STUMBLED into the kitchen bleary eyed. "Coffee?"

Maddox laughed and held out a cup. "I know better than to withhold it from you, love."

"Thank you," He mumbled as he took a big sip and turned to lean against the counter. He watched the news reporter Sicily give a live update on the tv. "Why are you watching a human station instead of one of the supe channels?"

"She's standing in front of the factory that was going to produce the chips Senator Dickhead wants to use on us."

Tristan was wide awake now as he listened intently to her broadcast. "Eyewitnesses called it into the fire department a little after four am this morning. Crews have been battling for hours to get it under control. The building is believed to be empty of workers. We'll keep you updated with this developing story as the morning goes on. Back to you, Chuck."

"They kill our activist, so we blow up their factory. This isn't going to end well. There's no way the humans won't retaliate again." Maddox said wearily.

"So you don't think there's even the slightest chance this was an accident?" Tristan knew it wasn't, but part of him had to ask anyway.

"Well, we do have pig shifters, so pigs really do fly. I guess that means we can't rule out that it's purely coincidental."

"Wait." Tristan demanded as he faced Maddox, "Pig shifters I get. But flying? Since when do they fly? What the hell, man?"

"I was just seeing how awake you were. We don't have flying pigs... yet." Maddox smiled over his coffee cup.

"There isn't enough coffee in the world to make me like you right now," Tristan grumbled as he refilled his cup and then headed back to their room to get dressed.

"You sure liked me well enough last night."

Maddox yelled at his retreating back.

Tristan rolled his eyes, "Liking your cock is one thing…" He whispered.

"I heard that!" Maddox called from the kitchen.

"Shit." Tristan cursed. He was never going to remember supes had super hearing and considering he did too now, you'd think it would sink in.

Forty-five minutes later, they were just pulling into the parking lot when Maddox spotted Vic standing outside the main doors. "Do you think he's waiting for us?"

Maddox shrugged. "Only one way to find out."

They parked and climbed out. Vic waved a note at them as they walked up. "Morning. I'm sure you heard the news about the warehouse that burned down overnight?" He said as he handed them the note and a small device.

Tristan nodded. "Yeah, it's all over the news. Depending on the station, what's being reported. Have you heard anything official?" He asked as he watched Maddox open the note and read it before looking up to Vic and nodding.

"Suspected arson, but we didn't need a report to tell us that. The TPD is handling the case for now. We're pushing to be involved, but so far they are stonewalling us," Vic explained as he looked around the parking lot. "I'm heading out to a meeting, so I wanted to catch you before I left."

Once they were alone, Maddox passed the note to Tristan.

Interview the rift jumper and the people who are helping them. Find out as much information as you can. This is a signal jammer, use it but beware we don't know what technology they have, so it may not be enough.

Tristan glanced at his watch. "Come on, we've got a few minutes before Mancini's agent comes in for his interview. I could use another cup of coffee and with luck maybe they'll be some pastries or something."

"I was thinking you could take the lead on the interview. You've been here long enough, and it's not like this is a grieving family member."

They made their way up to their office, greeting those they passed and listening to the gossip. All anyone seemed to talk about was the warehouse burning down. Not that Tristan blamed them. It was a big deal, and he couldn't deny that part of him was happy that it had gone up in flames. With luck, the place would be unsalvageable and it would set them back long enough that the courts could make a ruling on the whole implant thing before things escalated any worse than they already were.

"Morning," Josh greeted as they entered their pod and saw some of the team standing around talking.

"What's going on?" Tristan asked. "Looks like we're missing out on all the fun."

Jaylen nodded eagerly. "I was just telling these guys about Willow working with Ensley and the interesting time she's been having."

Maddox cocked an eyebrow. "Is it bad? Do we need to intervene?"

"No, she's fine. Willow just didn't realize how morbid Ensley's sense of humor could be. That and she apparently has a and I quote 'Unhealthy obsession with serial killers'."

"It's not unhealthy," Ensley announced as she entered the room behind Tristan and Maddox. "It just makes me a better agent. The more you understand them, the easier it is to catch them."

Jaylen nodded and then smiled devilishly. "So you don't have a 'shrine' to them in your house?"

Ensley laughed. "Is that what she called it? No, it's nothing like that. I have a lot of books about the different ones, and maybe a few are signed by the actual killers themselves."

Tristan gaped at her in shock. "Are you shitting me right now? You actually went to the prison they're locked up in and had them sign the books?"

Ensley cocked her head to the side. "None of you have ever done that?"

A chorus of no's and hell no's filled the air. Ensley shrugged. "I know we shouldn't give them attention, but it really does help to get inside their heads to help catch others."

"Exactly when did this fascination with these killers start?" Josh asked with a smirk, as if he already knew the answer to her question.

Ensley shifted as she glanced from person to person. "I think I was in middle school or so."

Tristan threw his hands up in the air. "Did she pass the psych eval for this job, or did she get to bypass it? Can we sign a petition to have her retested? I'm seriously wondering if we should be worrying about her."

"Not only did I take it... three times... but I passed it with flying colors." Ensley laughed at Tristan's look of astonishment.

"Seriously?" Tristan questioned in shock. "I was only kidding..."

Cole interrupted their banter as he let out a curse. "Guys, breaking news. Turn on the tv," He said as he pocketed his phone.

Sheppard grabbed the remote and flipped it to one of the local supe stations. The news anchor was trying to be serious as he announced that "Senator Richard Crump had been reported missing from his home shortly after six am. According to the police file, his wife reported when she went to bed at eleven he was in his home office working. An inside resource has told us that his wife reported that at three am when she went to check on him, he was gone. His phone was still in his office and no signs of foul play have been reported."

"Holy shit," Maddox mumbled. "This is bad. Like really bad. We thought it was getting crazy out there before. This is going to make everything so much worse." His phone dinged. "Vic just texted. They are hearing the Governor is considering a curfew and calling in the National Guard."

Cross whistled. "I guess they are expecting the worst, too."

"I'm not surprised. I'm sure you all have seen how things are getting more hostile out there. Hell, Maddox got hit yesterday as we were clearing the street so we could pass." Tristan waved to his partner in agitation. "After these two news blasts, I can only imagine how much worse it'll be."

Tristan glanced up at the tv. The news anchor was showing a picture of the activist who'd been killed two days earlier. "The city has asked organizers of the candlelight vigil to cancel. They don't want any large crowds gathering. The organizers have already released a statement saying they will not be scared into submission and the vigil will take place as planned."

"I assume TPD will be there. Would it be wrong if we showed up too? I know not all the TPD are racist assholes, but enough are that I worry what will happen." Tristan bit his lip as he glanced between the human cops standing there. "No offense to any of you, of course."

Jaylen shrugged as he patted Tristan on the back. "I agree with you, if that helps at all."

Josh nodded. "You didn't have the greatest experience with us, so you're justified in saying what you did. If nothing else, I say we go out unofficially to keep an eye on things and to show our support."

Maddox's phone pinged again. "Our guy is here. I'll go get him and meet you in the conference room.

Tristan made a pit stop in his office to grab a notepad and then followed Josh in to take a seat at the table. It only took a minute for Maddox to come in, followed by a short, overweight guy with a really bad comb-over.

"This is Agent James and Officer Bradley. Mr Sanders, please have a seat." Maddox gestured to the chairs as he sat beside Tristan.

"Please call me Bertie," the other man said as he pulled out a chair. "I was really hoping you were calling me in to give me good news, but that's not the case, is it?"

"No, I'm sorry." Tristan agreed, "We've recently taken over his case and wanted to double check everything. I appreciate you meeting us like this."

Bertie sighed as he placed his laced hands on the table. "Of course, anything I can do to help. Antonio was a good kid, a hard worker, you know. Everyone loved him. He was down to earth and for a model slash gym rat, that's kind of unheard of, you know."

"Can you tell us about the last time you saw him and if you had any idea what he was doing the day of his disappearance?" Tristan nodded as he doodled on his notepad to make it look like he was taking notes.

Bertie nodded, "I spoke to him a couple of days prior. I'd just lined up another gig for him, this one was with a big time photographer for a print ad. It was going to be a game changer for him. He was excited. We talked out the logistics, and that was it. The day before the shoot, he texted to confirm the time and location, but he never showed up. I went by his apartment, but it was empty. He wouldn't return my calls or emails. I checked with some of the other models he was friends with, but no one knew anything."

Tristan frowned as he tapped his pen on the pad of paper. "Did he live alone? Is there anyone who might know his day-to-day schedule?"

"Kids his age are all about social media. He Instagrammed everything, he worked out usually twice a day, went to clubs at night to be seen. When he realized a lot of human women were watching the videos of him lifting while his allure was turned on, he's an Incubus, you know, he made that his thing, and his followers skyrocketed." Bertie paused as he thought for a moment, "He was addicted to his phone and documenting his life. I follow him on all the platforms, but he hasn't posted since the night before. He looked happy. He'd just finished a work-out. He'd put a hashtag about new opportunities, but that was the only thing that stood out."

"New opportunities?" Tristan repeated.

"Yeah, he had the shoot the next day, you know.

At least that's what I assumed, but it could have been anything. He'd put stuff like that when he met someone new he was interested in, or if something different happened that he thought was a good sign."

Tristan glanced at Josh and Maddox with a raised eyebrow to see if they had any questions they wanted to ask. When neither man spoke up, Tristan turned back to Bertie. "Is there anything you can think of that we should know that wasn't in the original report?"

Bertie cocked his head as he thought and then shook his head, "Not really, he doesn't have any family. He's got a long list of acquaintances, but nobody that's really close to him. He grew up in the foster system. I discovered him dancing at a club that I happened to be at with another client and signed him on. He's pretty guarded about his past. He doesn't trust easily because of it either." Bertie sighed and looked at the three men, "I'm not stupid. I know the chances of finding him alive after three months are slim, but I have to hope that he's okay and you can find him and bring him home. He's a really good kid that deserves a break in life for once, you know."

Tristan nodded his understanding and stood up.

"Thank you for your time. If you think of anything, please give us a call."

Maddox stood and escorted Bertie out, while Josh and Tristan headed back to the office to write up their reports of the interview. It wasn't even lunchtime, and he was already exhausted.

CHAPTER
Fifteen

MADDOX DIDN'T KNOW if their phones were monitored, so he asked Ceka to meet at the food truck in Ybor. It was public enough and busy enough they'd be able to get away if someone did show up at the address.

Maddox parked and tossed his phone into the glove compartment. "Leave yours here too. Let's not risk it."

He grabbed the signal jammer and stuffed it in his back pocket and then jumped in line to grab lunch.

"I thought we were here to meet the lady?" Josh asked.

"We are, but you don't come here and not buy

something. Mrs Diaz would be devastated." Maddox said, exasperated.

Tristan looked at Josh and nodded. "You never want to insult Mrs Diaz. Her food is worth killing over."

Maddox's skin was crawling. He hated the idea that some secret agency could be hiding and watching them. He had to take the chance though, that they wouldn't have known the text had to do with the rifts.

"There are my boys. And you brought a new friend." Mrs Diaz called out as they stepped up to the window to order. "Are you hoping to distract me so I don't admonish you for staying away so long?"

Maddox rolled his eyes. "We were here five days ago and you know it."

"Yeah, that was so long ago. You both look too skinny. I don't think you are getting enough food when you don't come here."

Maddox patted his abs. "There is nothing skinny about my body. But you are right that five days was forever ago. If I don't get one of your Cubans I might actually die."

Tristan snorted. "You are so dramatic."

Maddox stuck his tongue out at him. "This is my church. Leave me be."

They ordered and snuck money under the tip jar since she never accepted money from them.

Josh grabbed a picnic table and waved them over.

Maddox set the sandwich in front of him. "Be ready for a life altering meal."

He stared at the man and waited for him to take his first bite. Based on the moans coming from him, he'd converted another person to join his obsession.

"We've been trying to talk her into moving into a storefront so she can serve more people, but she's stubborn and set in her ways. But with food this good, she deserves it and so much more." Tristan explained as he wiped his mouth with a napkin. "I'd eat here every day if she'd let us pay without resorting to drastic measures."

Josh mumbled his agreement as he devoured the food.

They finished and cleaned up so they'd be ready when Ceka arrived.

Ten minutes after their agreed upon time, Maddox was getting antsy.

Josh pointed across the street. "Is that her peeking around the side of the building?"

She made eye contact with them and darted out of sight. "Come on. Let's go to her."

The trio scanned every face as they passed. They turned down the alleyway she had been in and saw her standing ten feet in, partially hidden by a dumpster.

Maddox walked close and whispered. "Turn off your phone and give it to Josh. He's going to put it in our truck with ours until we're done. Is that okay?"

She hesitated for a moment and then handed it over. Josh took the phone and ran out of the alley.

"Thank you for trusting us." Maddox pulled the signal jammer out of his pocket and showed it to her. "I'm going to turn this on as a precaution. It'll make it so no one should be able to listen in on our conversation."

She nodded as her eyes darted in every direction. "I hate it here. I wish I could get my family and go back through the rift. I'll take risking starvation over this."

"We need to talk to the people helping you. Can you take us to them?"

She nodded. "They are waiting in a van back there. They said if you agree to drive around and talk to them, they'll meet with you."

Maddox looked at Tristan, who shrugged. "Fine with us." He glanced back and saw Josh coming down the alley. "He's back. Lead the way."

She hugged the walls and walked quietly. He gave her credit she was good at being stealthy.

A black van with heavily tinted windows sat idly on the side of the road. The side door opened. A man with golden eyes waved them in.

They got situated on the benches and waited until the van was driving. "Thank you for agreeing to meet with us."

The man nodded but didn't say anything.

"We want to help, but we knew nothing about this. We didn't know there were undocumented supes here or rifts opening, or secret police kidnapping them. How did you get involved in this?"

"I came through a rift five years ago. I was alone and had no one. Back then, there was no one hunting us. A couple of months after I was here, I heard some people talking in a bar about a weird light floating a few feet off the ground and they thought they'd seen people walk out of it. I knew right away they were talking about a rift. It took a while, but I found the family hiding in an abandoned building. Like me, they had no idea what they were doing or how they were going to survive. They said they had no choice but to take their chances here. Things were getting steadily worse on the other side." He paused as he slowed down to take a turn and then started up again.

"I didn't have much as I was still trying to figure things out, but I couldn't not help them. Together, we created a network of people, places, and businesses to help us help anyone else who came across. The bigger we got, the further we spread out, so we were ready to respond wherever the rifts opened. We have groups in nearly every state."

Maddox shook his head. "How the hell did we not know about this?"

The man smiled. "We wouldn't be very good at our jobs if you did. The whole point was to stay off the radar of anyone with authority."

"What changed? Why did you come to us now?" Tristan interjected. "I'm glad you did, don't get me wrong."

The man sighed. "It didn't take long for the soldiers to start showing up and rounding up those they could capture. We went from rescuing everyone to, if we were lucky, grabbing one or two. The rest are taken and never seen again."

Josh cursed, "And you have no idea who these soldiers are or where they're taking these supes?"

"We've gotten reports of them being taken to different military bases around the country, from there though they disappear." The man explained quietly.

"I know of hundreds of people who've come through over the years, but the number who are actually here are significantly smaller," Ceka announced into the silence.

"We keep meticulous records of all who enter, so we can help reconnect family and friends." The van driver explained.

Maddox nodded his understanding. "How do you know when a rift will appear and where it will be?"

"That's the issue, we don't. We listen to talk around town of sightings of weird lights, of people that don't fit in, and then we check it out. It's not a perfect system, but it's all we have."

Tristan frowned. "I'm going out on a limb and guessing the group the soldiers belong to have figured out how to track the rifts since they are rounding everyone up so quickly."

The man nodded. "That's our assumption as well."

Josh gave Maddox a pointed look and nodded to the jammer. Maddox sighed and cleared his throat. "I want you to understand we're going to do everything we can to figure this out and rescue your friends and family. But we need you to know that they are on to us already. We're taking every precaution. Our phones were left behind. We have this signal jammer and we're careful about putting things in writing or talking near technology."

The man cursed as his hands tightened on the wheel.

"You just need to be careful and keep an eye out." Tristan tried to calm the man down. "We wouldn't put you or your organization at risk. We took every precaution before coming today."

Josh cocked his head and studied Maddox. "You trust Mrs Diaz, right?"

Maddox nodded without hesitation. "Yes, without a doubt."

"Since we can't risk phones, how about if we need to meet up for any reason we have her put something on the menu that will alert the other party we need to meet up."

"Do we want to get her involved? This could be dangerous for her." Tristan questioned as he tapped his leg absently with his hand.

Maddox stared out the window for a few seconds before answering. "I don't want anything to happen to her, but I also know as an immigrant herself, she would help in any way she could. Hell, if we tell her about the network, she'll probably go broke trying to feed everyone. We'll just keep her in the dark as much as possible. She won't ask questions."

The man nodded and held his hand out. "Since we're going to be working together, I guess I can give you my name. I'm Rye. I have a good feeling about you all."

Each man leaned forward and shook Rye's hand.

"If you can drop us back at our truck, we'll get Ceka her phone and work out all the details with Mrs Diaz."

What the hell had they gotten themselves into? This was way above his pay grade, but his need to help people would never let him walk away from this. He'd do whatever it took to help them.

CHAPTER
Sixteen

THEY'D JUST ARRIVED BACK at the office
when Josh's phone buzzed with a breaking alert
message. Tristan turned to Josh. "I'm almost afraid to
ask."

Josh nodded, "No shit. But this isn't bad this time.
It's just stating that the Raymond James Stadium has
offered to allow the candlelight vigil to be held there
to help with safety concerns. They released a statement stating that as a human they support the
supernatural community and they feel everyone
deserves a place to mourn in peace without fear of
repercussions."

"Woah," Tristan exclaimed in surprise. "That will
help with security, for sure. Is it still on for tonight?"

"Yes," Josh agreed as he continued scanning the

article. "Seven pm, they will have enhanced security on site, it says."

Maddox chuckled. "They are going to get serious backlash from the human side."

Josh shrugged. "This is how things change. We need people on both sides willing to work together."

"Such an optimist. I've always loved that about you." Maddox teased him.

Josh whistled. "Update on the Senator... there isn't one. They held a press conference saying there were no signs of forced entry and the home security cameras had been shut off around two a.m. There have been no ransom demands or anyone claiming responsibility."

"Something tells me there won't be a ransom either," Tristan mumbled as they moved down the hall.

As they entered the pod, Vic walked out of his office and held up a piece of paper that simply said showers.

Tristan cocked an eyebrow and opened his mouth to make a smart ass reply, but quickly changed his mind. They were trying to be discreet, so as much as he wanted to make an innuendo, he'd have to let this one slide.

Maddox nodded and headed to their office to

drop off their phones before going to the elevators to go back down to the gym's lockers. Tristan glanced into the offices of the rest of the team as they passed and frowned as he saw they were all empty. It was early enough that somebody was usually still in office. Hell, he was pretty sure Reed pretty much lived in his office now. He couldn't remember the last time he'd seen him go home at a decent hour.

As soon as they entered the locker room, Tristan moved up next to Josh and whispered knowing that Maddox would hear him anyway, "I feel like it's a waste to even carry a cell at this point."

Josh laughed and nodded his agreement as they entered the steamy showers at the back of the lockers. Tristan shouldn't have been shocked to see the rest of the team there, but he was. It made sense they'd all want an update, but what would it look like if anyone came upon them all in there like this? He could just imagine the rumors that would fly through the agency over it.

"Now that we're all here," Vic announced as he came up behind them.

Kiely raised her hand. "Why couldn't we have done this in the women's showers? They are much cleaner and smell better."

Vic ignored her and moved on. "Tell us what you found out."

Maddox repeated everything they'd learned and the system they'd set up with Mrs Diaz.

"Anyone else feel like you're really shitty at your job right now because we didn't know about this?" Sheppard said.

Several of them nodded their agreement.

Vic shook his head. "You can't think like that. These people thrive on the secrecy and fear. It took that woman great courage to step up and inform us, especially when she didn't know if we were part of the group taking these people. I think the only thing we can do is make this public. Let the world know what's happening and bring the light to the darkness. There is only so much we can do alone, we need help. The red tape, and lack of knowing who exactly we can trust, ties our hands."

"What are you thinking, then?" Tristan asked in confusion.

"You guys made a contact while working on Quinn's case. I think we need to set up a meeting and have her expose it all."

Maddox nodded. "Sicily Bronson, she seemed decent and I have no doubt she wouldn't be scared away. Should we have someone from our side too?"

"Good point. I know a reporter. When you have a time and a place, invite me for dinner and I'll have him there."

Vic looked around at the assembled team and smiled sadly. "Okay, and while we're here, anyone that wants to attend the vigil tonight and help with security is welcome. I've talked to the owners at Ray Jay and they have welcomed us in to assist. I'll be heading there shortly to get the lay of the land and figure out the best way to assist. Who's in?"

Cross chuckled. "TPD must have been pissed when such a high-profile company offered to help out. Now TPD has to help with traffic. I personally can't wait to go."

The rest of the group expressed their agreement that they were attending. Vic smiled. "This is why our task force will make it and prove to anyone who doubted us."

Tristan opened his mouth to reply when he froze and turned to the shower opening. The rest of the Supes followed suit, while the humans looked between them in confusion.

"Shit, when did orgy Fridays start, and why weren't we invited?" Logan called out as he came around the corner and stopped with a smile while

Finneas stood beside him with a confused expression on his face.

Vic snorted and shook his head. "I swear I'm surrounded by people who think of nothing but sex."

Ensley raised her hand. "Um not true. I think about serial killers more often."

Tristan laughed. "Remember our earlier conversation? You've just made my point for me."

Vic turned to Finneas and Logan and studied the two of them. "What are your plans for this evening?"

Logan jerked his thumb at the Fae beside him. "I was just going to practice throwing this guy around the mats a bit. Why what's up?"

"We're going to the vigil to help keep an eye on things. You guys want in? We could use the extra manpower." Vic explained.

Finneas nodded, "Count me in." He winked at Logan. "You can toss me around another time, big guy."

Logan snorted. "Just tell me what you need me to do tonight."

Vic nodded. "I'm thinking that we need to split up and patrol. Tristan, Maddox, Finneas, and Kiely, I want you guys flying above and watching for anything suspicious. Jasmina, I want you to be our sharpshooter, just in case. We'll get you set up in the lights if we have to. But I think to be on the safe side, we need you and your eagle eyes." Vic waited for their nods of agreement before assigning the rest of the team. "I'm going to go between the gates. The rest of you I want split into three teams of four. One for each level. Stay in groups of two and patrol."

Tristan turned to Kiely. "Do you have a P.I.S. vest you can wear while you're shifted?"

"Nope. They just slap a sticker on my rump and I fly away."

Tristan glanced at Maddox to see if she was serious. Everyone was always fucking with him. It wasn't his fault he used to be human.

"Is she kidding?" Josh whispered to Tristan.

"You humans do know we have super hearing, right?" Kiely grinned as she turned to Josh and winked.

Vic rolled his eyes at their antics. "Yes, she has a vest she wears. All shifters have one for when they're in their non-human forms."

Lexi snickered, "So it's kinda like a dog harness. You know the ones that have their owner's name and number on them. But instead, this says P.I.S. Agent or something?"

Kiely flicked her off with a laugh, "You're lucky

I've gotten to know you, and know that you don't mean that as an insult, bitch."

Tristan smiled at their banter. No matter what happened tonight, this gave him hope about the future. With luck, tonight would be uneventful, but if not, he couldn't imagine having a better group of people at his side and back.

CHAPTER
Seventeen

MADDOX HATED BRINGING his wings out in public, and now he was about to fly over seventy thousand people. He glanced over and noticed Tristan's face had lost all color. "You okay? You don't look so good."

Tristan shook his head, "I've flown once, Maddox. Once. I'm not sure I'm ready for this and don't even get me started about trying to land with all those people around."

Maddox frowned. "I didn't think about that. We can ask Vic to ground you for this. One more person on the ground is a good thing."

"No, if he wants me in the air, I'll be in the air. I just need a minute to freak out. But I do have one very fucking important question."

Maddox raised an eyebrow in question.

"How do I get in the air? I had to jump from the platform. I don't know if I can do it from the ground."

Maddox tapped his finger on his chin as he thought about it. Teaching someone how to do something that was second nature was much harder than he expected. "I can take off from the ground, but that's because I've been doing it for years. We can take the escalators up to the top and jump off from there or you can have Kiely give you a ride up above the stadium and you just leap off her back."

"How is Jasmina getting up to the lights? She can't fly..." Tristan shrugged. "I guess jumping from the top will work. Will you do it with me again?"

Maddox grabbed him around the waist and pulled him close. "Baby, I'll be right next to you the whole time. I'll hold your hand the entire time if you want." He pointed to the side with his head. "And Finneas is giving Jasmina a ride up to the lights."

At that moment the fae took off from the ground with Jasmina and her rifle case.

Tristan nodded. "Okay. Let's head up."

They wound their way through the crowd as they went up to the third level. He found a quiet corner that faced outward and jumped up on the ledge. "Okay. Let's do this."

Tristan blew out a breath and climbed up beside him. "This gets easier, right? I don't want to have to hold your hand for the rest of my life just to do what comes naturally to you. I feel like a failure as a shifter, if that's the case."

"You're a baby shifter. Give yourself a break. And if you want to hold my hand for the rest of our lives, I'm happy to do it." He held his hand out and waited for Tristan to grab it.

They released their wings at the same time. Maddox smiled at Tristan. "See, that used to be hard for you, but I don't have to smack your ass anymore, at least for that. You'll get this in no time."

Tristan laughed, "Promise me you'll never stop smacking my ass, at least when we're alone at home. In public... yeah, I can do without that now."

"As you wish. Now let's get up there before this starts. One, Two, Three,"

They dove outward and turned upward when they caught the wind stream. Tristan had a huge smile on his face. "Feels good, doesn't it?"

Tristan nodded. "I didn't realize how different it would feel. It's so much better, I can feel the currents in the air. Like my body instinctively knows what to do and how to make it work to my advantage."

"Exactly. You just need to learn to trust yourself. Are you ready to let go or want to stay holding hands?"

"Babe, I never want to let go." Tristan smiled at him. "But yeah, it'll probably make us look unprofessional if I stay latched on while we're supposed to be patrolling."

"I just got a really dirty image in my mind of you latching on to something of mine. I've never done that while flying... something to consider for another time."

"Wait, is that even possible? You know what? Don't answer that right now. But we will be coming back to that later."

Finneas flew by at that moment. "Hey, guys. Looking good Tristan. Logan said you were great the other day."

Tristan shrugged. "I don't know about that. Maybe good at landing on my face, but I did fly so there's that."

They were interrupted when Kiely flew between them, sending them fluttering backward. Now that Lexi called the vest a dog harness, it was all Maddox could see.

"Would it be wrong to say how adorable she looks with that on?" Tristan questioned softly after she'd flown away.

Maddox gave him a serious look. "I wouldn't get on her bad side. Empaths can feel everything you do. Unless you want her broadcasting every time you get turned on or scared by something."

"No wonder you treat her so well. With your previous man whore ways, she must have been on overload with you."

He shrugged. "I'm not sure. I would hope she could block us out when she needed to. Otherwise, I have a lot of apologizing to do."

The crowd below them screamed and clapped as a woman walked on the stage in the center of the field.

Her voice echoed across the stadium as she gave an impassioned speech about what a great man the activist was and everything he wanted for the future of supernaturals and humans alike.

Jasmina's voice came across their earpieces. "Can someone on the first floor go check out the pirate ship? I think I saw a glint of something."

"On it," Cross answered.

They watched below as Cross and Raelle wound

through the crowd toward the pirate ship. Finneas flew down and stood on one of the masts.

"That area is like twenty thousand square feet. Can someone else get there so you guys can clear it faster?" Vic's voice came across.

"Reed and I are circling in from the other side," Cole answered.

Maddox and Tristan continued to circle above as they kept an eye on the crowd while listening for any updates on the pirate ship. It was a tense few minutes until the all clear was given.

Another forty minutes passed by while people went on stage and gave speeches about the man and the cause. Maddox had tried to get Tristan to land several times to take a break, but the stubborn fool refused. This was a long flight time for him and he'd been doing it for years. He was about to find out how good Tristan's pain tolerance was.

Tristan glanced around for Kiely and found her on the grass outside the stadium. She'd already shifted out of her animal. He called her name over the earpiece.

"Yes?"

"So, I um... well, I don't really land well yet. Would it be totally embarrassing to ask for your assistance in getting my ass back on the ground so I don't have to crash land again?"

She laughed. "I don't know... Maddox, is it okay if your boyfriend rides me?"

Maddox rolled his eyes. "He doesn't usually want to ride your team, but if he wants to switch it up, I won't say anything."

Tristan rolled his eyes as laughter filtered through the earpieces, as the rest of the task force had a good laugh at his expense. "I hate you all."

Kiely shifted back and took off toward him. She hovered near Tristan and waited for him to climb onto her back.

Maddox grabbed his cell phone out of his pocket and took a picture. Tristan could kill him later.

"The stands are almost clear. Finneas, you can bring Jasmina down." Vic ordered.

Everyone met back up near their cars. Maddox ripped his vest off. "I am so glad that went well. I really wasn't holding out any hope it would."

They all agreed as they took off their own vests and talked amongst themselves for a minute.

Maddox elbowed Logan. "Do you mind dropping Josh back at the office? I need to take my boyfriend home and get him in an ice bath."

Logan glanced over and saw Tristan tensed up as

he leaned against the truck. "Yeah, looks like you're going to have a rough night. Have fun with that."

Maddox walked over and opened the passenger door of the truck. "Come on, babe. Let's get you home."

Tristan let out a pained whimper as he climbed in. "Why didn't you tell me about this part of it? And where the hell can I get some muscle relaxers?"

"Dude, I told you it's been years since I've had to think about this stuff. And technically, I did tell you to take a break a few times, but your stubborn ass refused." Maddox smiled as he closed the door on him and went around to the driver's side.

"I didn't want to be the weak link. No one else had to take a break." Tristan pouted.

Maddox reached across the bench and grabbed his hand. "I get that and I'm sorry you're going to have a rough night. I know everyone appreciates you hung in there. You are the strongest baby shifter I've ever met."

Tristan snorted, "Well yeah, because all the other baby shifters are actual babies."

Maddox threw his head back and laughed. "I was trying to give you a compliment, but you got me there."

CHAPTER
Eighteen

TRISTAN STRETCHED and let out a groan as his stiff muscles protested. "I thought the ice bath was supposed to help, and you told me as a supe this shit would go away. You lied."

"Would it have changed anything if you'd known? And really, it's a great excuse for me to have to give you a lot of massages all weekend, right?" Maddox whispered in his ear as he rubbed Tristan's shoulders.

He was just getting into it and starting to relax when his phone rang with the tone he'd set for his mother's facility. Instantly, the tension built back up in his back as he reached for the phone with a shaking hand. Every time they called, it was because something had happened. She was having more bad days than good and he was scared that soon he'd lose her and be alone in the world.

"This is Tristan." He answered the phone hesitantly.

"Mr James, this is Janice Caffrey. I'm the head nurse on the overnight shift and I was calling to inform you of an incident that occurred overnight with your mother."

Tristan rolled over and sat up. "What happened? Is she okay?" He could hear the tremble in his voice, but didn't have the strength to hide it right now.

"Physically, yes, she is fine. She had an episode and attacked one of the nurses. We had to restrain and sedate her for everyone's safety." Janice replied carefully.

"The nurse, is she okay?" Tristan frowned as he realized this could be the last straw and they finally tell him she had to move into a safer environment with people who can handle her.

Janice cleared her throat. "Yes, she's fine. A bit shaken up, but otherwise she's good. We've put a call into your mother's doctor to ask him to come and check on her. Is there a way you can come down so we can talk in person? There are some things we need to discuss."

Tristan blew out a breath of frustration. "Of

course. When can we meet? I can be there whenever it is best for you."

"Thank you, I appreciate that. I'm here for another two hours, and then I'll be back tonight at seven," Janice explained with a clinical detachment that left Tristan feeling cold.

"I can be there in thirty minutes." She thanked him and hung up. Tristan sat there feeling lost as he contemplated how this day had gone so far off the rails so quickly.

"I'll go get dressed unless you'd rather go alone?" Maddox asked.

Tristan shrugged as he stood up. "It's fine. You don't have to go. I'm sure there are things you have or want to do. There's no reason for you to suffer through this, too."

Maddox reached around and grabbed his chin, forcing him to tilt his head back and look at him. "I'm never suffering when I'm with you, and this is part of being in a relationship. If you want or need me, I'm there. If you want space, I can give you that too."

He really wasn't sure he could handle going there alone and seeing her in this condition, but he hated to drag Maddox into his family problems. He felt selfish for asking him, but he just wasn't sure he was strong enough without having him to lean on. "I need you. I don't think I can do this alone. She's all I have left, and I'm losing her so quickly."

He pulled away and headed into the bathroom to hide for a minute while he regrouped. He hated feeling that vulnerable. Asking for help was not easy, especially when you were used to doing things alone.

When he came back in the room, Maddox was dressed and sitting on the side of the bed. Tristan smiled at him shakily and moved to grab his own clothes. Time was always against them, it seemed.

"Do you want me to make you a coffee for the road?" Maddox offered.

Tristan shook his head, "I don't think it's a good idea with how sick to my stomach I am right now. I just want to get this over with and face whatever fate is throwing at me next."

He knew he was being ridiculous, but he couldn't help the irritation he was feeling at Maddox. He'd poured his heart out and admitted he needed him. He made himself vulnerable, and all he had to say was, I'll make you coffee for the road. What the hell was that?

He threw on his clothes, grabbed his wallet, badge, and gun, and headed to the kitchen, where he grabbed a bottle of water and some ibuprofen. Fuck this day already.

Tristan pulled up outside the home where his mother lived and put the truck in park. The trip over had been silent, and that only seemed to piss him off more. Being in his head was the last thing he needed right now. Sure, Maddox was with him physically, but he felt miles away right now. He got that being in a relationship was new, but come on.

"Fuck me," He grumbled as he climbed out of the truck and headed up the walkway. He felt like he had the sword of Damocles hanging over his head and no matter what he did, it wouldn't go away.

The receptionist greeted them as they walked in and told them that Ms Caffrey would be right up to get them. Tristan thanked her and moved to the little lobby area to sit and wait. He lasted a minute before he was up and pacing again. He could hear the sounds of the residents talking, the clink of the silverware on plates, and the quiet murmurs of the staff as they moved around them all.

It felt like forever before Janice Caffrey appeared in the doorway with a gentle smile. "Mr James, I'm

Janice. I'm sorry we're meeting under these circumstances. If you'd like to come back to my office, we can talk there."

Tristan nodded and followed after her. The nurses and orderlies nodded as they passed. He'd forgotten how friendly this place was. It was one of the reasons he'd picked it in the first place. They had a reputation for being caring, devoted, and had excellent ratings from all the reviews he'd read. It was pricey, but worth it for his peace of mind. If they kicked his mom out, he didn't know what he'd do or where he'd be able to find a place as good as this one.

"Have a seat." Janice motioned to the two chairs in front of her desk.

Tristan sat, "Ms Caffrey, this is my partner, Maddox Smith."

Maddox nodded a greeting, which she returned. "Thank you for coming in so quickly. Let me start by telling you I adore your mother. On her good days, she is an absolute sweetheart. A favorite among the staff and residents alike."

Tristan smiled. That was the mom he knew and remembered. She'd never met a stranger.

"On her bad days, which I'm sure you're aware are becoming more frequent, she can be a handful. It wasn't until recently, though, that her violent outbursts have become the norm. I'm afraid in the section that she resides in, we're not equipped to handle that behavior anymore."

"How long before I have to get her out of here?" He asked in a resigned tone.

Janice shook her head, "No, I'm sorry you misunderstand. She's not leaving. I'm just suggesting we move her to a more … specialized area." She paused as she glanced between the two of them. "The only downside of this is that it costs more and is a bit restricted on visiting hours. But in return she gets more individualized round-the-clock care and we have nurses and staff that can handle her behavior without putting any undue stress on you or your mother."

Maddox reached over and squeezed Tristan's thigh. "This is good news and I can help with money if it's an issue. We're in this together, right?"

Tristan bit his lip as their words revolved around in his head. This was a lot to take in at one time. Maddox's touch was keeping him grounded, something he desperately needed right then. "Ms Caffrey," He paused as he tried to think of how to ask what he wanted to know. "I'm not a doctor or know much about medicine or anything like that, but from what little I've researched, this is a bad sign, isn't it?"

Janice's eyes softened in sympathy as she nodded her agreement. "I'm afraid so. This is the best-case scenario for your mother. She'll get the best care we can give her and you'll be kept in the loop every step of the way. I know this is hard, so if you need time to think it over, we can arrange that."

Tristan nodded absently as he gripped Maddox's hand and squeezed. No matter what he was going to do this, he'd do anything for his mother. "I don't need to think, yes of course we'll move her. Do I need to sign papers or ..." He shrugged helplessly.

"Not right now. We can handle that later. Why don't you go see your mom and we'll get everything set up? She was sleeping, but she might be awake now, and from past experience, she usually has a few good minutes after an episode. Take advantage while you can."

Tristan nodded and stood up and headed back into the hall to see his mother and the future that was coming a lot quicker than he'd ever thought possible.

Maddox stopped Tristan before he went into the room. "If you want to skip the bachelor party tonight

to hang here with your mom, Silas would understand completely."

"No, I think it would be good to get out of my
head for a while. And my mom won't know I'm here,
anyway. I'll take these few good minutes and hold on
to them. It has to be enough for now."

He pushed open the door and smiled as he saw
her sitting up in bed watching tv. "Hey, mom."

She smiled and held up a hand, beckoning him
closer. "Tristan, hey baby."

CHAPTER
Nineteen

MADDOX WISHED for the hundredth time he didn't have to do the bachelor party. Not because he didn't like them, but because it meant spending an entire evening with his dad's fae friends. People he'd actively pushed away his entire life. He wouldn't blame them if they shunned him now.

Silas brushed his beautiful silver hair off his shoulder. "Thank you again for not planning some cliche crazy night. I love Quinn, but sometimes her human side really shows."

"Should I take offense to that?" Tristan joked.

Maddox snorted. "I think we've tainted you enough. I don't think there's any human left in you."

"I'm not sure that's a good thing," Tristan muttered.

Maddox shook the nerves from his arms and grabbed the door. He could do this. He could be friendly.

In the corner of the room was a group of impossibly gorgeous men. When they saw Silas, a cheer went up, causing everyone in the place to stare at them.

They wound their way through the pool tables. The fae pulled Silas in for hugs, then surprisingly hugged Maddox and Tristan as well.

Silas' best friend, Renfell pulled Maddox to the side. "I'm so glad to see you with your father. I always knew the two of you would get your relationship figured out."

Maddox didn't know what to say.

Renfell continued on. "You were always such a quiet boy, keeping to yourself. I love hearing the stories about you now and everything you are accomplishing with the agency. Your father is so proud of you."

"Thank you, sir. And for what it's worth, I'm sorry I was always such a moody asshole when I was there. I know you never slighted me. I was just going through some shit and didn't know how to handle it." Maddox's stomach flipped. Why was he saying so much? He hadn't even started drinking yet, and he was already oversharing.

Silas walked up and flung an arm over Renfell's shoulder. "Have you met my son's boyfriend yet?"

Renfell held his hand out to Tristan. "And very handsome, too. Nice catch, Maddox."

Maddox was going to tease Tristan later. He always thought his father was gorgeous and now another beautiful fae was complimenting him. He was probably flying on cloud nine from the comment.

Tristan blushed and stammered a thank you and nice to meet you, causing both men to laugh.

The group grew silent when another fae walked in and straight up to Maddox. Why the hell had he been invited?

Maddox glanced at his father, who gave him a wink. He did this on purpose.

Maddox cleared his throat. "Matthis, it's good to see you."

The fae held his hand out, but wasn't smiling. "It's good to see you."

Silas and Renfell backed away. At least Maddox wouldn't have an audience for this. "Tristan, this is Matthis. He was my neighbor when I was at my dad's. He's also the one I punched in front of all the neighborhood kids because I thought I had some-thing to prove."

Matthis eyebrows rose halfway up his forehead. He must not have expected Maddox to own up to what he did. Obviously, Silas brought him here to help him fix all the shit he'd done as a kid.

Matthis reached out and shook Tristan's hand. "It's nice to meet you. Your boyfriend was all the talk when he was in town. All the girls and some of the boys wanted to date him."

Maddox's jaw dropped. "Seriously?"

Matthis chuckled. "Did you not know? I think it was all those muscles of yours. You're exotic compared to us boring fae."

Maddox's mind was blown. How wrong he'd been about everything. Did this mean he had to get over his issues with Finneas now? Was he wrong about him, too?

Matthis nodded at them and walked away.

Tristan laughed at the gobsmacked look on Maddox's face, "So you could have started your man whore ways at an earlier age if you'd known that."

Maddox's jaw dropped. "That's what you got out of all that?"

Tristan shrugged. "Well, he did say they all wanted you. What else was I supposed to take out of that? That my man is a sexy beast. I already knew that."

Maddox shook his head at him. "Here I am mending fences and building bridges and all you can think about is how hot I am. You are obsessed with me." He kissed Tristan before he could respond and went to get a round of shots for everyone.

He came back with a tray and passed one out to each person. "Thank you all for coming tonight. You've been there for Silas even when I wasn't, so I thank you all for that. My parents have been in love my entire life and I had been blind to it. I am so grateful they have taken this next step. My mom deserves to be happy and there is no one else in the world who could do that better than him. To Silas." He held his glass up. Everyone repeated 'To Silas' and drank their shot.

Tristan gasped as he looked at Maddox, "What the hell was that, and where can I get another one?"

Maddox shrugged. "I just asked for the most potent shot they had. After the week we've had and what's coming, I figured we needed a little help loosening up and forgetting our problems for a while."

"I'm not complaining at all, but you do remember the last time you had to carry my ass home, right?" Tristan smiled as he waggled his eyebrows.

Maddox cupped his hand behind Tristan's neck and pulled him close. "I'll carry you home any night, even if you aren't drunk."

"You say the sweetest things," Tristan leaned in and kissed him. "How about before you get me drunk and take advantage of me, we challenge your dad and Renfell to a game of pool? Losers have to do a dare of the winners' choosing."

"You have that much faith in your skills to agree to an open-ended dare?" Maddox asked.

Tristan smirked, "I plan on buying your father and Renfell lots of shots to make sure they won't win. I play to win, baby."

"I like your style. Hey Dad," Maddox called out.

Maddox cackled as he held on to Tristan. Their plan to get Silas and Renfell drunk backfired, and all of them were completely trashed.

Lucky for them, they had still managed to win the pool game and had dared the fae to fly up to the billboard of the Governor and draw a mustache and devil horns on his face.

The men had readily agreed, and somehow they'd gotten themselves to the sign. Maddox and Tristan stood on the ground, watching the fae work. Or trying to, Maddox's vision kept going in and out of focus.

"Hey, do you see pretty flashing lights everywhere or am I hallucinating?" Tristan asked.

They turned and found three police cars pulling to a stop in front of them. "I think we're busted." He looked up at his dad. "Fly away. They can't get you. Be free." He sing-songed.

Unfortunately, the two men were so drunk they'd barely made their way up there and now couldn't figure out how to get down.

The officers surrounded them with their hands on the hilts of their guns. "What's going on here?"

Tristan giggled, "We're just standing here, officer. No law against that."

The officer in front of him pointed at their hands. "And those cans of spray paint you're holding are the same color as those two up there are using. Is that a coincidence?"

"They dropped them." Tristan exclaimed, "We were just picking them up for them!"

Another officer walked up. "Those two up there

are stuck. We're calling a ladder truck to come get them."

Maddox tilted his head to look up and nearly fell backward, except one of the cops caught him. "Dad, I said to fly away. What are you doing?"

Silas was on his stomach, looking down at them. "I won't leave you. We're in this together." A second later, vomit flew from his mouth and rained down on everyone below.

Tristan gagged. "Oh no. I'm a sympathetic puker." He bent over and threw up in the grass.

"Mother fucker." One of the cops yelled from behind them.

A fire truck pulled up. The firefighters took one look at them and burst into laughter. Two of the cops handcuffed Tristan and Maddox and tossed them in the back of their squad car.

They watched as the ladder was raised and Silas and Renfell were carried down while they sang 'I've got a lovely bunch of coconuts'.

Tristan laughed as he turned to Maddox. "Best bachelor party ever."

Maddox sighed and leaned his head on Tristan's shoulder. "I agree, and did you know you stink?"

The officers got in the car and ignored them the

entire drive to the precinct. Apparently, they didn't like being vomited on.

Maddox was dragged out of the car. "If you take my wallet out of my back pocket, you'll see I'm a paranormal federal agent. Don't call my boss though. Can you call my mommy instead?"

"Call his mommy for me too," Tristan begged as he was brought up next to Maddox. "I'm an agent as well."

They were thrown into a cell and joined by Silas and Renfell a few minutes later.

"Why didn't you fly away?" Maddox asked Silas.

Silas leaned close. "I can't feel my wings... I think they're gone." He turned around and his wings were fluttering fine.

Tristan giggled, "They're numb. That's so awesome. How did you manage to fly like that in the first place?"

Silas shrugged. "Did we fly up there? I was wondering how we got there."

"Why didn't you portal away?" Maddox asked.

Silas gasped. "I totally forgot I could do that!"

Renfell plopped onto the bench. "Why is it every time I'm with you Silas we end up like this?"

Maddox's jaw dropped. "You've been arrested for being drunk in public before?"

Silas sighed dramatically. "Once or twice. This plane is so prudish. In the fae plane, we can be free with our frivolity, but these humans just can't handle a good time."

"It might have had something to do with you puking all over us, too. People tend to frown on that after all." Tristan explained helpfully.

"What in the hell is going on in here?" Vic demanded as he came around the corner and glared at the four of them.

"Vic," Silas greeted enthusiastically. "You missed the party. Where were you?"

Vic raised his eyebrow as he got a good look at the group. "I think it's a good thing I did now."

Tristan sighed and turned to Maddox and mock whispered, "They called him anyway. Daddy's mad." Then burst into laughter.

Vic groaned and shook his head at them all. "Public intoxication, defacing public property and you're damn lucky they aren't charging you with assault on an officer." Vic made eye contact with each of them until they dropped their eyes in shame. "Silas, you are old enough to know better. What example are you setting for your son and Tristan?"

Tristan nodded eagerly.

"And don't get me started on you two." Vic

rounded on Maddox and Tristan. "You are federal agents, and yet you stood there and watched these two idiots destroy property."

Maddox held up his hand. "We weren't actually watching. I couldn't see two feet in front of me, so technically, you're wrong there."

"And I'll have you know the whole thing was their idea to begin with." Silas jumped in.

Tristan gasped, "You traitor!"

Vic rubbed his hand down his face with a pained sigh. "For the love of everything good in the world, shut up all of you."

"They're free to go." An officer walked up with a frown on his face. "But they will be

expected to pay for the billboard to be replaced."

Vic nodded his agreement and stepped back so they could leave the cell. "Let's go. I'm taking all of you home, where you will stay until the morning when you're sober. We'll discuss your actions then."

Silas and Renfell linked arms and went back to singing as they followed the agents out of the building and to Vic's SUV.

He turned and glared at them. "And you'll pay to have my car cleaned because you're going to ruin the upholstery after this."

The drive to Marta's house was silent except for

the older fae's random singing. Maddox had never met such happy drunks before.

Vic pulled into the driveway and turned off the car.

All five men saw Marta at the same time. She was standing at the front door with her arms crossed. Tallie and Quinn were standing behind her with stupid grins on their faces.

Maddox shook his head. "No way am I going in there. I don't even live here. Drop them off and you can take Tristan and me to our place."

"Son, I heard you asked for your mommy at the station. Here she is." Silas said with a wave of his arm.

They all jumped when someone knocked on Maddox's window. He jumped back to see Marta's frowning face an inch away. Thank god the glass was between them.

"Tristan, you go out first. She won't kill you," Maddox whispered.

"What the hell? You're my boyfriend and senior agent. You're supposed to keep me safe, not throw me to the wolves."

Vic growled. "Anyone not out of this car in thirty seconds will be up at six a.m. scrubbing that billboard personally."

Maddox bit his nail. "I'm not sure that's worse than getting out of this car."

Vic glared at him.

"Okay, okay. Geez." He opened his door. "Mommy, you look beautiful tonight. Did you get your hair done?"

"Don't mommy me." She snapped as she took them all in. "What did you all do? I expected this type of behavior when you were a teenager, but you're all grown ass adults. I'm ashamed of you all."

Maddox winced and pointed to Tristan, "It was his idea."

Tristan gasped, "Traitor. You're both traitors. It's a family trait, isn't it?"

Maddox leaned close. "I love you, but someone has to take the fall, and she likes you best."

Tristan was going to make him pay later but it was worth it to keep Marta from yelling at them in the front yard while they were starting to come down from their buzz. Tristan loved him. He wouldn't hold a grudge.

CHAPTER
Twenty

TRISTAN ROLLED over with a groan as he snuggled into Maddox's side. "They're doing it on purpose, aren't they?"

Maddox tried to laugh, but ended up moaning in pain, "Probably."

"I can't wait to return the favor one day," Tristan said as he closed his eyes to block out the bright light. "I swear I didn't know people could make that much noise."

A loud knock on the door made them both groan again as Marta stuck her head in the door and called out loudly, "Get your lazy butts out of bed. Lunch is on the table."

"I used to like her," Tristan complained as he felt Maddox huff out a laugh. "The only good thing about this whole thing is we can go home and hide. Silas is stuck here."

Maddox shook his head and climbed out of bed. "You better hope neither of them heard you say that or there will be even more hell to pay. You already accepted the blame last night, so you're on her shit list, remember?"

"Yeah, about that." Tristan glared at Maddox as he sat up on the edge of the bed. "Way to throw the love of your life under the bus, man."

Maddox shrugged. "Survival instinct kicked in."

They dragged their feet as they made their way to the dining room.

"Morning!" Tallie screeched.

"You guys look like hell," Quinn shouted.

Maddox groaned. "Why are you guys so loud?"

"Marta, one day when they come home drunk, you have to let us know so we can return the favor," Tristan grumbled as he dropped into a chair at the table.

"Ha. We're not that irresponsible. We had the bachelorette party last night and look at us. We're absolutely fine. You are the heathens." Tallie teased.

Tristan narrowed his eyes at the two teens. "Yeah, but did you have as much fun as we did?"

Tallie laughed, "You call being dropped off at the

house of your boyfriend's mother in the middle of the night covered in vomit fun?"

Marta set down a platter of sandwich meat way too loudly. "All my children bickering like they are toddlers. Tallie, Quinn, give the boys a break. It's not their fault they don't always think with their brains like we do."

"Hey, Silas and Renfell were there too. How come you're not giving them a hard time?" Tristan demanded sullenly.

"I will, but they don't bounce back quite as well as you do. They are still passed out cold. You forget they aren't as young as you." She scolded.

Tristan shrugged, acknowledging the truth of her words as he grabbed some bread to make a sandwich and soak up some of the alcohol. You'd think he'd remember how potent the damn drinks were and take it easy. But nope, they tasted too damn good. That or his boyfriend was just a really bad influence.

Maddox got serious as he grabbed Marta's hand. "I'm sorry. I shouldn't have put Silas at risk. We just had a terrible week, and I really needed to let go. It's been years since I've been that drunk. I forgot how out of control I can get."

Marta smiled at him as she patted his cheek

gently, "I won't say it's okay, but I do understand. When we talked, I could hear the fatigue and stress in your voice. You know, if there is anything we can do, you just have to ask."

Quinn nodded. "And I'm sorry too. I know all this craziness is because of my father and what he did to me. I hate that his choices are burning the world to the ground now."

"This isn't on you in any way." Tristan patted the teenager's hand. "You were a victim. Nobody blames you. And as for the world, things have been getting progressively worse for a while now. They were looking for any excuse they could find."

"Okay, enough about all of this. Eat up and let's talk about something better." Marta grinned as she sat down. "Like the fact I'm getting married in less than a week."

Tristan winced as the girls all squealed in excitement and talk turned to the upcoming events and what still needed to be done. He tuned them out as he got lost in his head with all that they needed to do.

"Hey, can I borrow one of your phones for a minute?" Tristan interrupted the conversation about the rehearsal dinner.

Marta nodded as she handed over her phone. "Did something happen to yours?"

"No, I..." He trailed off and looked to Maddox, unsure of how much to say. "Ours are dead. We didn't think to borrow a charger last night."

He took the phone and stood up. "Excuse me for a moment, please." He didn't need to leave the room to send the text message, but he needed to get the number from his cell and didn't want anyone to know he'd lied about the battery by pulling it out at the table.

He found Sicily's contact information and entered it into Marta's phone. He turned his phone off and moved into the bathroom so he could turn on the shower to help block any sound, just in case. Once he was sure he'd done as much as he could, he hit dial and waited for the reporter to pick up the phone.

"This is Sicily."

"Hi, this is Tristan James, with P.I.S." He paused and waited to see if she would remember him since they hadn't spoken in a few months.

"Yes, Agent." She replied with a smile in her voice. "I'm surprised to hear from you. What can I do for you today?"

Tristan licked his lips as he hesitated for a

second in doubt. "Can you meet us at Froggy's tonight by any chance?"

"I can make that work." She replied slowly.

"Don't bring any electronics, including your phone. And be careful, please." Tristan blew out a breath, "Don't tell anyone about this. We'll explain tonight. No texts or emails about it either. I promise this is worth your time, but we have to be careful."

She paused for a moment and then finally said, "I'll be there at seven. Will that work?"

"Perfect." Tristan agreed readily. "We'll see you tonight." He hung up, turned off the shower, and headed back to the table. He handed Marta her phone and gave Maddox a small nod to let him know it was done.

They ate their lunch and shared details about the night before until Marta glanced down at her phone and smiled. "Well, it looks like your boss is calling to check up on you boys." She said as she hit answer, "Morning Vic."

Thanks to their shifter hearing, they could all hear his side of the conversation. Tristan and Maddox groaned as they heard his first words. "Are Tampa's most wanted agents up yet?"

Marta laughed, "They're sitting here glowering at

me as we speak, actually. Silas and his cohort are still recuperating, though."

Vic snorted. "No surprise there. They aren't spring chickens anymore. Any chance I could talk to one of them?"

"Sure," she handed the phone to Tristan since he was closest.

"Hey boss," He greeted with a shrug to Maddox. He'd freaked and hadn't known what to say.

"Hey boss?" Vic repeated. "That's all you have to say after I was woken up at two am to come bail you two out of jail?"

Tristan winced. "Um, thank you, boss?"

"That's a bit better," Vic grumbled.

"What if I tell you we have a report for you if you want to meet us for dinner tonight at Froggy's at seven?"

Vic hesitated for half a second. "I can be there."

They made small talk for another moment and then hung up. Tristan thanked Marta as he went back to his sandwich, even though his stomach was now tied up in knots. Things were getting real now. There was no turning back for better or worse the world was going to know about what was happening. He had to hope they were making the right decision.

CHAPTER
Twenty-One

MADDOX GRABBED the keys to Scarlet. "Can we take my car? No offense to your truck, but I really miss my girl."

"I don't mind. My truck has been getting a lot of action this week. It'll be nice to have a break and we don't want Scarlet thinking we're playing favorites after all." Tristan put his cup in the sink and called over his shoulder. "Josh is meeting us there, right?"

"Yep. Message was delivered and I think he understood the code. I just wish we could have changed the meeting to somewhere else. I'm not sure I'm ready to smell alcohol again this soon." At the thought, his stomach rolled.

Tristan laughed, "Hair of the Dog and all that, right?"

Maddox gagged. "Absolutely not. Have at it, but that's never worked for me."

They hopped in the car. Maddox smiled as he revved the engine. God, he loved Scarlett.

As they drove to Froggy's, they were forced down different roads than usual, as more and more barricades had gone up to separate the two communities. TPD wasn't able to keep up with clearing them before more would pop up.

Froggy was standing at the bar, watching for them when they entered. "There they are. I thought you were my best customers than I heard you cheated on me at a different bar. That hurts."

Vic sat on the other side of the bar, smiling at them.

Maddox rolled his eyes. "You only have one pool table and we had a bunch of people. Now I wish we had come here. You would have cut us off long before we got that trashed, and you definitely wouldn't have let us leave like that."

"You're right, though I can't say I'm upset by what you did to our lovely governor's face." Froggy grinned at them. "When you want a drink, the round is on me for that alone." He wiped the bar absently. "I heard about the special requests tonight and it's not a problem. Go ahead and take your favorite booth."

They nodded and made their way to the far corner booth. Vic joined them and sipped a glass of whiskey as he smiled at them. "Would you like some?" They both made gagging sounds. "Didn't think so."

The door to the bar swung open. A man they recognized from tv walked in, saw Vic, and came their way. "Long time no see. Man, when you do something you do it big, don't you? I can't wait to hear what's going on."

Vic laughed. "Good to see you, Mick. Maddox, Tristan, this is Mick Mahoney."

They exchanged handshakes.

"You left your phone outside, right?" Vic asked.

"Yes sir. I'm free and clear."

The door of the bar opened and Siciliy walked in with Josh right behind her.

Mick whistled. "Interesting. Now I really want to know what's going on."

Sicily waved as she sat in the booth. "This looks like a fun party."

"Sicily, I don't believe we've officially met. I'm Victor Judge, and you know my agents Tristan and Maddox."

Vic pointed to Josh. "This is Josh Bradley. He's part of our new human-paranormal task force. Josh, I'm sure you've seen Siciliy on tv and know her, but you may not know our other friend. Mick Mahoney, he's a reporter on one of our local supe channels."

They all exchanged greetings as Maddox pulled out the little black box and turned it on. "The signal jammer is on." Vic waved his hand at Froggy, who turned the jukebox on as loud as it could go.

The group in the booth huddled close.

"Thank you guys for coming, even though we made bizarre requests." Vic started, "We have become aware of something going on in the government and we think you are just the people to help us bring it to light. As we were made aware of what was happening, our phones were hacked and we were sent a message warning us to back off. If this sounds too intense and you want to leave now, we won't blame you." He waited for a second. When neither reporter moved, he continued on. "A woman came to us and told us there were still people living in the paranormal realm and they were starving to death. A few years ago, rifts started opening, and supes from that side came through. They set up a network all over the country and have been helping new rift jumpers, as we call them, to acclimate over here."

Both reporters were writing furiously in their notebooks.

"This woman had jumped the week before, along with her husband and kids. Soldiers were waiting for them. She managed to get away, but everyone else was taken. The team met with the leader of the network for this area. He confirmed the soldiers started showing up a couple of years ago. Often right as the rifts were opening. They estimate thousands of supernaturals have been taken. They tracked them to military bases, but don't know what happened to them after that."

"What the fuck?" Mick said softly as he jotted down notes. "And you said years, right? I didn't miss hear you. You said it's been going on for years without anyone knowing about it?"

Maddox nodded. "At least five years, from what we can tell."

"And what exactly do you want us to do?" Sicily questioned as she studied each of their faces.

"Help us investigate who in the government might be doing this. Who has the power and connections to run this super secret group?" Vic said.

"But remember, you have to do this low key," Tristan emphasized. "They've already proven they are monitoring us. They are making thousands of people disappear. They won't think twice about a couple more."

"Not to mention how many people might be waiting to jump. They've lied to us all this time. We were told there was nothing left on the other side. How many people have died while we're living free over here?" A vein in Mick's forehead pulsed.

"We've set up a way to contact the underground network helping the refugees. We can set up a meeting with them if you want or need it. But it has to be kept on the down low. They are scared and if too much attention is brought to them too quickly, it could derail everything they've set up," Tristan explained.

Vic pulled four phones from a bag beside him and handed one to Maddox, Mick, and Sicily. "These are essentially ghost phones. It's untraceable and not connected to any of us in any way. Use these to keep in touch. No calls, texts only, understood?"

Everyone agreed and then sat there in silence as they stared at each other, taking in everything they had learned. Vic sighed, "We didn't bring you guys in lightly. We trust you and I'm not sure if I should apologize for that or not." He smiled to show he was joking. "But seriously, be careful out there. If you run into any trouble, come to us and let us help. We'll feed you any information we uncover and we just ask that you keep us in the loop as well."

Sicily and Mick nodded as they put their phones in their pockets.

"When it's time, Sicily and I will break this story together and show the world that we can work together for the betterment of all of us." Mick offered his hand to Sicily to shake in agreement.

"You're damn right we will." She agreed without hesitation. "Be safe everyone. I'll be in touch." She stood up and headed out of the bar with a nod of thanks to Froggy as she passed him.

Mick left next. As soon as he was gone, Froggy cut the music.

Maddox blew out a breath. "We're getting pretty good at this clandestine stuff. I think we're ready to be spies next. I've always thought 007 was hot." He knew he probably shouldn't joke, but the weight of what they were dealing with was overwhelming.

Josh cocked his head and studied Maddox and Tristan. "Why do you two look like death warmed over tonight? Rough weekend?"

Vic grinned. "You could say that. These two idiots decided to get drunk and deface public property and then get arrested."

"And you didn't call me to witness them in the drunk tank?"

Maddox didn't appreciate their humor. Even worse was how bad the office was going to be. The whole team likely already knew and were going to give them hell when they got back in the office. He just wanted one night to relax. Even that couldn't be easy.

CHAPTER
Twenty-Two

"WHAT'S ON THE AGENDA TODAY?" Tristan asked with a yawn as they walked into their pod and froze at the sight of all their teammates standing there. "What's going on?"

Vic smirked as he moved to the front of the group. "Nothing. We were just filling each other in on our weekends."

Maddox groaned as Tristan narrowed his eyes at Vic. "You didn't."

Josh grinned, "He did."

"I hate you all." Tristan said as he flicked them off and headed to his office. "Assholes," He yelled as he saw the piles of spray paint cans on their desks.

"Where did these come from?" Maddox

demanded as he pulled a picture off the wall. "They didn't book us, so how did you get photos?"

"We work for the TPD and still have friends over there." Jaylen called out with a grin.

Josh nodded. "Plus, we have a genius hacker who can get anything off their computers..."

"Cole... I thought we were friends." Maddox asked.

"We are," Cole agreed. "And this is what friends do, right?"

"Yup," Sheppard nodded. "If we can't make fun of each other than are we really friends?"

Vic held up his hands with a smile. "Okay guys, fun's over. I've got some things to discuss with you all." He waited for everyone to find a seat around the table. "I know things are progressing rather slowly in our missing persons cases and that's to be expected with so much time having passed. We need to keep working on those. Jasmina, Kiely, Willow, do you guys have anything to report on the assassination case?"

"Frustratingly slow," Kiely reported with a shrug. "TPD is working with us begrudgingly, but so far, we're hitting nothing but dead ends."

Lexi raised her hand. "We did finally locate the sniper's nest, though. Forensics is going through it with a fine-tooth comb. They are pretty sure it was a human shooter. Though that is of no surprise to anyone."

Vic nodded. "Okay, if anything changes or you need assistance dealing with them, let me know."

The three women nodded and Vic moved on. "The powers that be are being very tightlipped about the abduction of the Senator. Their lack of leads, and with the Senator being who he is, I have no doubt we'll discover this was an attack by a supe. When it comes out, things will escalate even more. As you've all probably noticed, the streets are becoming hazardous. Both sides are fighting over territory and blockages are going up left and right."

The group broke out into murmurs as Vic raised his hand to quiet them down again. "I know you're all busy, but be ready because we'll be called in to help as the TPD gets overwhelmed. Also, it's come to my attention that tomorrow, with it being a national holiday, the humans have decided to hold a 'pride parade'. There is chatter in the supe community of crashing it. We've been asked to attend undercover and try to keep things peaceful alongside the TPD. Don't let anyone instigate trouble and make sure you are all on your best behavior. We don't need to give anyone any ammunition to use against us, understood?"

"Now they need a fucking human pride parade? Isn't every day about them already?" Reed slapped his hand on the table. "No offense to the humans in the room, of course."

Vic shook his head at him. "It's not our place to decide what they can and can't do. Our job is to keep our side from showing up and turning it into a riot. Now, enough grumbling, you all have cases to work on. Get to it."

Tristan stood up and headed back to their office. He could feel Maddox and Josh on his heels. They still had four missing cases, and no leads on any of them. He dropped into his chair and grabbed Antonio's case file again. "Does anyone have Instagram, so we can check out the Mancini kids' account? See if there is anything on there to help us?"

"I was actually thinking about him this weekend." Josh turned in his chair to face them. "The agent, Bertie, said the kid lived in an apartment. He's been missing for a few months, so what happened to his stuff? Was the kid paid up, and it's still waiting for him to return? I mean, that's not very likely, and if he had no family…"

Tristan shrugged and grabbed his phone. "I

hadn't thought of that. Let me give him a call and see what he says."

"Hey Josh, I'm still waiting for Mrs Bates to call me from Italy. Want me to look into anything with one of the two you're looking at?" Maddox asked.

Josh handed him the Lopez file. "I'm digging into the messages from the fake family to Maria. Can you check the national databases to see if there have been any hits on Lopez?"

Tristan hung up his desk phone. "Okay, Bertie packed his apartment up. The landlord evicted him a month after he disappeared for non-payment. He's having the laptop couriered over today. He said he could have the boxes brought by in a couple of days if we didn't mind waiting as he was headed out of town again."

"Nice," Maddox mumbled absently as he stared at the computer screen in front of him.

Tristan dug his phone out of his back pocket. "Holy shit. We need to go." He held his phone out for Maddox to see.

It was a text from Tallie saying Quinn had collapsed and they'd rushed her to Shifter General.

They jumped up and asked Josh to let Vic know what was happening as they raced out of the office and down to Tristan's truck.

Maddox turned on the rarely used emergency lights. "You get us there. I'll text we're on our way."

Even as a trained agent, it didn't help the feeling of fear and dread Tristan felt as they drove the fifteen-minute route to the hospital.

"Tallie says she's up in ICU and Obinski is with them." They raced through the hallway and up to the unit. Tallie stood in the hall with her hands bandaged while Marta held her and rubbed her back. Silas was next to them with his hands and arm bandaged as well.

They skidded to a stop next to them. "I thought Quinn collapsed. What happened to you guys?" Maddox was white as a sheet.

Tallie pulled out of Marta's arms and into Maddox, who gave Tristan a look of utter bewilderment.

Marta wiped a tear from her cheek. "We were in the kitchen baking. Quinn was bent over, pulling a pan out of the oven, when she suddenly stood up and then collapsed to the ground. She was convulsing on the floor. Her hair... it turned black and started to shrivel up. Tallie was trying to see what was wrong, but Quinn's body was so hot it burned her. Silas came in, opened a portal, and had to hold on to her long enough to get her here."

Dr Obinski walked out and closed the door behind him. "Afternoon. I don't think Quinn is in any immediate danger."

The group visibly wilted with relief.

"I'm running tests, but my hypothesis and that's all I have with her case is that her Phoenix genes tried to push forward. Her hair is growing back as we speak. I think it was a sort of rebirth like Phoenix go through just slightly altered because she is only partially one. If this is what is happening, I can't promise it won't happen again. The dragon bone marrow is stabilizing her, but that doesn't mean sometimes her other genes won't try to take the lead. Honestly, it's going to make her one of the most interesting supernaturals in the world."

Tristan grimaced. "I'm not sure an eighteen-year-old girl wants to be the most interesting."

"You're probably right. She's stable if you want to go in." He shook hands with them and went on to the next room.

Maddox knocked gently and called her name.

"You guys can come in," Quinn called.

Seeing her in the hospital bed brought back memories of how they first found her.

"I'm so embarrassed you all came down here."

Marta waved her off and walked over to brush

the peach fuzz on top of her head. "None of that now. Are you okay?"

Quinn nodded but stopped when she saw Tallie and Silas' bandages. "What did I do to you guys?"

"Oh, this, it's nothing. More importantly, we lost all the cupcakes, so when you're back home, we have to start over." Tallie teased her.

Quinn gently touched her arm. "Seriously. Did I hurt you?"

"You did nothing. I just couldn't handle that hot body of yours. But don't worry. Dr Obinski put some medicine on it and said we'd be better in a day or two."

"You guys are too good to me, all of you." Tears poured down her face. "I've been nothing but a hassle."

Tristan squeezed her blanketed foot. "I've learned with this family they will be there for us no matter what. We lucked out with them taking us in, didn't we?"

Maddox grabbed Tristan's hand and squeezed.

"Hey kid, you know when you're up to it, we should practice flying. I'm tired of being the only adult 'baby supe' learning to fly. We can do it together."

Quinn grinned up at him and nodded eagerly. "I'd like that a lot."

"Maybe we should go swimming sometime too, check to see if your mermaid lungs work like theirs do. We need to figure out what you can do, right?" Tristan winked at the kid.

"Ooooh. She got some werewolf too. Should we give her some raw meat on the full moon?" All four adults looked at Tallie like she'd lost her mind. "Geez, sorry, I was trying to help."

Quinn laughed, "I didn't take offense. I thought it was funny."

Tristan shook his head. Who would have thought the two of them would end up being such good friends? They'd both been through hell in their young lives. It was nice to see them acting like teenagers for once.

CHAPTER
Twenty-Three

THE SUN WAS SETTING as Maddox and Tristan left the hospital. Quinn was doing great and Obinski planned to release her in the morning. He'd been so scared when he saw that text. He'd only known her a short time, but she was just as important to him as anyone else in the family.

He rolled his head to the side and looked at Tristan. "Do you ever just feel absolutely weary? Like everything is shit and there's no release? I mean, we've been having shitty days at work, and our off time seems to be almost as busy. As soon as possible, we need to book a vacation somewhere far away that is off grid. I want to unplug from everything and just be with you. Does that make sense?"

Tristan nodded, "Yeah, it does. And I agree.

We've been going non-stop, and it's all high intensity, so it wears you down. As for the vacation, I say hell yes, sign me up. Can we find someplace where we can get a beach bungalow and clothes are optional? We can spend our days lazing on the beach and the nights in bed, making each other moan."

"We might have to go to another country for that, but it sounds perfect to me." He sighed as he looked out the window. "You know what else sounds perfect? My boyfriend taking me home and making me forget all of this. We're always rushing, tearing each other's clothes off. Can we try slow and sensual?" He reached over and grabbed Tristan's hand. "I've never made love before. It's always just been sex. I want my first time with you."

"No pressure there." He laughed softly. "But yeah, I'd like that. Though I like anything with you, if I'm being honest."

Maddox felt exposed admitting that, but if you couldn't do that with the person you loved, did you really love them? He'd known he could admit that to Tristan and he would support him and understand. He might tease him, but he did it out of love and not to be mean.

"Babe, are you ready to go inside, or do you want me to leave you here to think for a bit longer?"

Maddox grinned sheepishly as he opened his car door. "Sorry, I was in my head for a minute there."

Tristan nodded, "I get it. You don't have to apologize. Are you hungry? Do you want me to get us some food?"

"I'm good for now. Later, we can reheat some of the leftovers or order something if you want. Right now, all I want is you." Maddox climbed out of the car and waited for Tristan to join him on the sidewalk. He laced their hands together and headed inside, anticipation and nervousness warring for dominance in his body. He unlocked the front door and stepped inside. "So, what now?"

Tristan leaned up and placed a gentle kiss on Maddox's lips. "Now, you relax and let me take the lead. I want this to be special. I want to show the man I love just how special and amazing he is."

"Babe, I already know you love me and I don't ever doubt that. I don't need anything special, though. You are enough."

"Humor me on this." Tristan stepped back and winked as he pulled Maddox down the hall.

Tristan pushed him to sit on the edge of the bed, as he moved to stand in between his spread thighs and tilted Maddox's head so they were eye to eye. "I feel like it's Christmas and I get to unwrap my favorite present."

Maddox snorted, "You do realize you've seen this 'present' a lot already. And it's not like my body has changed."

"No, but it's sexy as hell and every time I see it I thank the fates for giving you to me," Tristan whispered against his lips as he kissed him. "Now hush and let me undress you."

Maddox bit his lip to keep from smiling at his gorgeous boyfriend's intense look as he slowly unbuttoned Maddox's shirt and pushed it off his shoulders. He shivered as Tristan followed the path with soft kisses, licks, and gentle nips of his teeth.

"I said slow and sensual, not to tease me."

"It's all part of my plan, now hush and let me do this." Tristan winked as he pushed Maddox to lie back on the bed. "The only thing you're required to do is lift your hips so I can get these pants off in a minute."

He wasn't sure it was in him to just sit there and do nothing, but for Tristan, he'd give it his best shot. He relaxed into the bed and focused on the places his mate was touching him. The heat of his hands as they traced their way down his chest and abs, the licks of his hot tongue in the dips and valleys everywhere and nowhere all at once.

He felt Tristan pull at the button of his pants, and then the soft whirl as the zipper was lowered before Tristan mouthed at his dick through the cotton of his boxers.

"There's my delicious present." Tristan gave a throaty moan of desire.

Maddox shifted as he attempted to use his left foot to remove his right shoe.

"I got it. Don't get impatient on me now." Tristan scolded playfully as he dropped to his knees and took Maddox's shoe into his hands. "You even have sexy feet. Did you know that?"

Maddox laughed as he leaned up to look into Tristan's eyes, "You are so fucking weird, but I love you anyway."

Tristan shrugged, "I'll take that as a win, then."

Once both of Maddox's shoes and socks were removed, he felt Tristan lean back. Maddox waited as patiently as he could, but the anticipation was killing him. "Tristan?"

"Sorry, I was just taking in the view." He winked as he leaned up and grabbed Maddox's jeans and boxers. "Lift up now."

Within moments, he was naked as Tristan tossed the last of his clothes over his shoulder to land on the floor behind them. He felt oddly exposed again as he lay there bare, with Tristan's eyes roving over his body.

"Move up on the bed and lay down in the center on your back."

Maddox nodded and quickly did as he was told. At this point, he wasn't sure he cared what Tristan told him to do as long as he touched him soon. His skin hurt. He was so desperate to feel his hands on him again.

"That's it, love." Tristan murmured as he climbed to his feet and quickly undressed himself. "If I could paint you, it'd be a masterpiece, but then I'd never be able to show it off because I'd kill anyone who saw the perfection I get to enjoy."

Maddox laughed at his cheesy lines, "I can promise from now on you're the only one who gets to see all of me in all of my glory."

A year ago, he'd have thrown up at just the thought of saying something like that, but now he couldn't imagine his life any different. Tristan was worth this and so much more, and he vowed to make sure he knew just how much he loved him every day.

CHAPTER
Twenty~Four

TRISTAN HAD to bite his lip to keep the moan from escaping as he grabbed the bottle of lube from the bedside table and dropped it onto the bed at Maddox's hip. He couldn't remember ever being so turned on as he was right now, knowing his mate was letting him control things tonight. It was a heady feeling and he could see why Maddox got off on it.

He was the master of Maddox's pleasure tonight. He got to decide what he did, where he kissed, sucked, and nibbled. A thousand thoughts ran through his head as he tried to figure out what he wanted to do first.

"Stop staring at me and do something. I swear I said slow, not glacial."

Tristan grinned as he climbed up on the bed at

Maddox's feet and stared up at him through his eyelashes. "There's so much of you to admire and explore. I got sidetracked in my fantasies, but you're right because the reality is so much better."

He ran his hand up Maddox's calf and up his thigh, skirting around his very erect cock and back down the other leg.

The moan that filled the air gave Tristan a thrill. He leaned down and nibbled and kissed his way up the path his hand had taken moments before. As he got to Maddox's pelvis he paused and placed a soft kiss on his leaking tip before moving up his stomach to trace his happy trail with his tongue and finally to his nipples.

"Are you sensitive here?" he asked as he licked one while twisting the other. He laughed as Maddox jerked and moaned, "I'll take that as a yes, then."

"Bastard." Maddox's grumble broke off as Tristan sucked the nub into his mouth and flicked it with his tongue.

"Holy shit." He groaned as he thrust his hips against Tristan, looking for friction.

"Not yet, I'm not done exploring you yet," Tristan whispered as he moved to give the other nipple the same attention.

He smiled as he felt Maddox's hands grip his

head and pull him against him. Yes, his man liked this, and he loved knowing he was driving him insane. He pulled off with a pop as he climbed up higher so he could look into Maddox's eyes. "Hi."

"Hi." Maddox smiled as he leaned up and pressed the lips together.

The soft kiss quickly morphed as Tristan traced his lips with his tongue, demanding entrance which Maddox happily supplied. Their tongues brushed and dueled as Tristan fought to keep the kiss slow and lazy. He pulled back and straddled Maddox.

"Can I ride you like this? I want to see you as I take you inside of me."

Maddox nodded eagerly as he grabbed the bottle of lube. "Do you want me to prep you?"

Tristan nodded, "Please, that way I can have my hands free to touch you." He leaned forward so Maddox had access as he laid kissed down his neck and chest. He tweaked Maddox's nipple and let out a laugh at his indrawn breath.

"That feels so good," Maddox moaned.

"Do I need to stop so you can get me ready? Or can you do two things at once?"

Maddox growled as he popped the top of the lube, "don't you dare stop."

Tristan rocked against Maddox's stomach and

pelvis, "Then you know what to do. I want to make you fly with me, baby."

He didn't have to say anything else as he felt Maddox's finger probe at his hole. He relaxed as much as he could to give him better access. He leaned down so he could whisper into Maddox's ear. "I love feeling you inside me."

Maddox nodded, "I love being there too. Ride my fingers baby, show me you're ready for my cock."

Tristan whimpered as he felt Maddox push three of his long fingers into his tight channel and began pumping. He loved this part of sex, the stretch and burn, the feeling of fullness he got when Maddox filled him up. "I'm ready. I need to ride you."

Maddox pulled his hand away and kissed Tristan before he let him sit up.

He lined himself up over his hard cock and slowly lowered himself down, staring into Maddox's eyes the entire time. "Don't close your eyes, baby. Look at me, I want to see you."

Maddox nodded as he bit his lip. "Love you so much."

Tristan smiled as he felt himself bottom out on Maddox's cock. He laced their fingers together as he slowly began to rock. He did his best to keep it slow and steady, but it felt so good and knowing that

Maddox was watching him intently just made the pleasure that much more intense. He knew he wasn't going to last long, he just needed to get Maddox there first.

He clenched his ass muscles off and on, heightening the sensation and tightness Maddox would feel. "You're so fucking big," Tristan whispered between clenched teeth as he fought back his orgasm. "I'm going to come all over your chest without you touching my cock."

"Yes." Maddox groaned as he thrust up into Tristan, "Fuck me, baby. God, I love you so much."

Tristan felt the familiar tingle building in his lower spine. "That's it, baby. I'm coming. Come with me, please."

Maddox didn't need any prodding. He squeezed Tristan's hands, stared into his eyes and shuddered in relief as he filled Tristan's ass with his cum.

"That was amazing." Maddox gasped as he pulled Tristan down for a deep kiss. "You were amazing."

Tristan smiled. "You amaze me. Thank you for giving that to me and trusting me to make that good for you."

CHAPTER
Twenty-Five

RAELLE WHISTLED when she looked at Maddox. "You are glowing. Did you have a good night?"

Maddox felt heat rush to his cheeks. He focused on pouring coffee instead of looking at her. "I don't kiss and tell."

"HA! Since when?"

He glared at her. "I'm taking this coffee to my boyfriend."

As he passed the window, he looked at his reflection. He wasn't glowing, was he?

Tristan and Josh were standing in the center of the pod with the rest of the team. Maddox handed them each a cup.

Vic came out of his office. "All right. You all know

your assignments. Have your ID ready, but try to blend in and pray to whatever you believe in that this doesn't turn violent."

He led them down to the parking lot and split them into two vans. Other teams from other pods were doing the same. There were probably going to be more agents there than human police. That probably wasn't a bad thing.

As they got closer to the parade route, the streets got busier. "Okay, I don't think I expected this many people," Tristan commented absently as they passed by, looking for a parking spot. "And did you see some of their signs? I can't believe I used to be one of them." He muttered in anger. "What the hell is wrong with people?"

Vic pulled the van into a parking lot that was cordoned off for official vehicles. They all climbed out and stood together. Vic looked them all over and gave a nod. "Be careful. Stay together in groups of two for safety and please call out if you need help or see anything."

Maddox sighed as he nodded to Tristan and they headed out to join the streams of humans making their way to the parade route. He kept his head on a swivel as he took in everything. He had to struggle not to let his disgust show on his face as he read the signs and saw the slogans on the shirts some of the humans wore.

"This is disgusting," Tristan whispered softly enough that only Maddox's shifter hearing would pick it up.

Maddox nodded as he tapped Tristan and pointed to a barricade they were coming up to that blocked a side street. "Protesters are already lined up over here." He called out over his mic to the rest of the team.

"Here too." Cross agreed.

The rest of them chimed in with similar reports.

"There's no way this is going to end peacefully with this many here." Tristan muttered as he did his best to walk among the crowd, ignoring the ignorant comments and hateful things he was hearing from the humans.

"What the hell is that?" Maddox growled as they approached a man with a cart full of flags. "There's a fucking line for that bullshit."

"What is it?" Vic asked in his ear.

Maddox winced as he realized he hadn't turned it off, so his words had broadcast to the whole group. "A vendor selling the American flag, but it has some alterations to it. It says 'Human rights are the only rights'."

"I've got a vendor down here selling t-shirts that say 'humans were here first'," Derek announced in disgust.

"Shit," Vic cursed, "It gets worse guys. I just passed a float that has stuffed animals hanging from nooses and a sign that says 'Death to supernaturals'."

"There is no way this isn't going to get violent." Tristan fumed.

Maddox's hands shook with rage. Thank god he didn't have a gun in his hand or who knows what he would have done. These people had crossed the line. "Why the fuck are we here protecting these people?"

"We're not. We're protecting the supernaturals who are going to show up and see this," Vic replied. "Change of plans. All teams converge on the side streets with the blockades. We're going to do our best to make sure the two sides stay separate. There is no way this isn't going to blow up and we need to be ready."

Maddox and Tristan shared a look and turned around to head back to the nearest blockade. He reported their location and then waited. Within a few minutes, Finneas and another agent came to stand beside them.

"Is it okay if we join you? This was the closest one to where we were at," Finneas explained.

Tristan nodded, "Of course." He held out his hand to the other agent. "I don't think we've met. I'm Tristan."

"Nice to meet you. I've heard of you." The man shook his hand with a smile. "I just wish it wasn't under these circumstances. I'm Lincoln." He pointed toward Maddox. "I assume that makes you Maddox. I heard you guys don't go anywhere without the other."

Maddox groaned. "Is that really the office gossip about us?"

Lincoln grinned. "That and more, but I'll save that for a less volatile time."

The steady stream of humans grew louder the closer they got to the start time. Paranormals stood at the gates behind the agents, yelling at the humans. As someone with a bullhorn started the chant 'Human rights are the only rights', the paranormals started shaking the gates.

For a while, it was under control, with both sides yelling but keeping to their own sides. It wasn't until one of the stuffed animals with a noose was being tossed around did a brick come flying from the paranormal side and hit someone Maddox couldn't see.

All hell broke loose. Both sides jumped the gates with fists flying.

A woman holding her baby was getting shoved around. Maddox ran over and covered her until he could get her away from the crowd. "Go home. It's not safe."

She nodded and took off.

Canisters of tear gas were fired above the crowd, but people weren't separating. In his earpiece, everyone was yelling about various fights they were dealing with. The violence had spread from one end of the parade route to the other.

"Shit, Willow is hurt bad. I'm getting her to the hospital." Sheppard called out.

Maddox would have offered to fly her, but Sheppard's vamp speed would be just as good.

He glanced to his left and saw Tristan holding two teenagers apart as they tried to swing and kick at each other. His blood ran cold when he found Finneas. The Fae was fighting off two guys. A man walked up behind him with a gun aimed at his back. Maddox didn't think. He ran toward them and jumped between the gunman and Finneas as the gun went off. The bullet hit him in the vest. He grunted as he went down.

The shot was loud enough to send people scurrying.

Finneas dropped to his knees. "Maddox, what did you do? Are you okay?"

His ribs burned, but he rolled to his feet and got up. "The bullet hit my vest and being part ogre, I can take a hit a lot better than you. I'll just have some bruising."

"Babe, are you okay? I heard the shot and saw you down." Tristan raced over panicked, "Let me get an EMT, or Finneas, can you fly him to the hospital?"

"Both of you stop. I'm fine. Let's help TPD finish clearing the streets, okay?" He hated being the center of attention.

Tristan and Finneas exchanged glances and then grudgingly agreed.

"Everything's calmed down here now. I'm giving the van keys to Cole. I'll head to the hospital to check on Willow and see you all back at the office." Vic announced through the earpiece.

Josh walked up with a TPD officer next to him. "Everybody good here?" He asked as he pulled the cuffed gunman behind him. "Is this the guy who shot at you?"

Maddox nodded. He had to fight the urge not to punch the man so hard his jaw shattered.

Josh smiled. "Okay. I'll get him in a cruiser."

The young officer looked panicked as he realized he was alone with a bunch of paranormals.

Maddox felt bad for him. "What do you need us to do?"

The kid looked really unsure about talking to them. "I was told to get the gates up and tell everyone to leave the area. Anyone who refused was to be arrested."

"Sounds fun. Let's see if anyone wants trouble."

"After that, I sure hope some do," Tristan grumbled as he grabbed one side of the fallen barricade.

An hour later, they regrouped at the vans and headed to the hospital. Finneas pulled Maddox to the side as everyone else went inside.

"Thank you for doing that. It was stupid, but I do appreciate it."

Maddox shrugged. "You would have done the same for me and probably looked a lot more graceful, too."

Finneas gave him a big smile. "Did the great Maddox Smith just tease me?"

Maddox blew out a breath. "Yeah, about all that. I had a shitty childhood, most of which was my fault.

I had a huge chip on my shoulder toward all Fae. I've always treated you unfairly, and you didn't deserve it." He held his hand out. "I'm truly sorry and will do better in the future."

Finneas looked at Maddox's hand, then opened his arms wide and pulled him into a hug. "I never took it personally. You are a great man and I look forward to being friends." He let go and walked into the hospital.

Maddox hadn't mentioned anything about friends, but when building bridges he shouldn't be surprised the other man was quick to cross it.

CHAPTER
Twenty-Six

"IT'S BEEN A FEW HOURS. Have you heard anything?" Tristan collapsed into a chair beside Sheppard.

He shook his head. "Not since they agreed to check her out and not try to send her away. I didn't think about her being human and just came here. She was bleeding bad, and it was..." He shrugged as he looked around at everyone. "I hope I didn't make things worse by coming here."

Tristan put his arm around Sheppard's shoulders and gave him a side hug. "You got her help, that's what counted."

They lapsed into silence as they watched people come and go from the small waiting room they sat in. Every time a nurse or doctor walked in, they all jumped to their feet, only to be disappointed when they called for someone else.

"I just got a text that Quinn is being released." Maddox waved his phone to Tristan. "I told them we were down here and what happened."

Tristan smiled. "That's good news. I wonder if Dr Obinski is still around. Maybe he can get some answers for us."

Maddox nodded as he typed a message and hit send, "Let's see if he answers."

Within ten minutes, Silas, Marta, Quinn, and Tallie appeared in the doorway. Marta raced over and gave each of them a hug. "How's your friend?"

"We don't know yet." Maddox shrugged and then winced.

Tristan frowned. If and when Obinski showed up, he was going to make him check Maddox out. Getting shot even with the vest on hurt like hell.

Maddox hugged Quinn, "How you doing, kid?"

"I'm good, tired. They don't let you sleep much in here. But I feel fine and look, my hair is almost completely grown out." Quinn smiled as she ran her hand through the short locks.

"Silas, Tallie, how are the burns?" Tristan noted their bandages had been removed.

"We're doing much better. The salve the doctor

224

gave us healed it up nicely." Silas rotated his arm to show the clear skin.

They made small talk for a few minutes until they couldn't ignore Quinn's yawns anymore. "Let us know how she is and if you guys need anything." Silas hugged them both goodbye and followed the group out.

"They really do look like a real family," Tristan said absently as he watched them leave. "A ragtag, odd family, but yeah, a family for sure."

Vic came over a few minutes later and sat next to Maddox. "I got a report that one of my agents was hurt. Why didn't I hear this from you?"

Tristan smirked at a glowering Maddox. "I was going to have the doc check him out, even though he says he's fine. I've caught him wincing a few times."

Maddox scowled at him. "I'm fine. I live with a fantastic nurse who will be happy to take care of me like I did for him after flying. I don't need to be seen."

Tristan bit his lip as he remembered just how well Maddox had taken care of him. But if his boyfriend had bruising on his ribs, sexy times would be a bit hard until he healed. That didn't mean he couldn't go down on him and make him feel good, though. He smiled as he made plans for later that were only interrupted when Dr Obinski came in with a spare scrub top and handed it to Sheppard.

"Thought you might want to get out of the bloody shirt. Even the strongest vampire can only take so much temptation, right?" Dr Obinski smiled at him before stepping back and taking the group in as a whole. "I checked in on Ms Parks, and you'll be happy to know she's doing fine. She has a concussion and a rather large laceration on the back of her head, as well as a few small ones on her forehead and arms. Head wounds bleed profusely, so that's why it looked as bad as it did."

Sheppard let out a breath of relief as his shoulders dropped. "And she's okay. I didn't make things worse by bringing her here, right?"

"No, you didn't," Obinski reassured him. "We were closer than the human hospital anyway, so I don't blame you for coming here. And with tensions as they are, who's to say they would have let you in?"

"Hey Doc," Tristan called, stopping Obinski from leaving. "Can you check out my stubborn ass boyfriend here? He took a bullet tonight, and he's in pain."

Maddox stood up and pulled his shirt off. "Everyone, take a good look. It's just a bruise. I'm fine. By tomorrow the bruise will be gone and if it's not, I'll agree to get checked out. Got it?" Someone in the back wolf-whistled. "Not why I did that, but thank you."

Tristan rolled his eyes but grinned up at his gorgeous man. "I'm holding you to that."

Dr Obinski turned to Vic with a laugh. "Never a dull moment with this group is there."

Vic nodded emphatically. "You have no freaking idea." He paused as he pulled his phone out of his pocket. "Any chance you can assist us one more time before you get back to work? Willow's fiancé just arrived, and he's human, so he's having a bit of a problem getting in to check on her."

Tristan frowned. "That's bullshit. Just because we're supes doesn't mean we don't have human friends and family. Anybody should be allowed in to see the patients."

Dr Obinski nodded his agreement. "One day, hopefully, that will be the case. Hell, in a perfect world, we wouldn't have segregated hospitals either. For now, we'll just do the best we can with what we have." He turned to Vic. "Let's go get him and I'll escort him back to Ms Parks. I'll make sure he has no more issues."

Vic started to leave and then stopped and faced the group once again. "It's been a long day. Everyone go home and rest up. We'll reconvene in the morning and write up incident reports then. Sheppard, good job today getting Willow taken care of."

Tristan stood and grabbed Maddox's hand. "I think I owe you a bit of TLC when we get home, big boy."

As soon as they walked in the front door, Tristan pushed Maddox towards the bedroom. "Go get a shower and I'll get us some dinner."

He watched his boyfriend with a smile as he stumbled down the hall. They may heal fast, but that didn't mean they felt no pain. Just that it went away quicker than it would for humans.

Tristan rummaged through the fridge and freezer looking for something to cook. He was hungry now and didn't want to wait for takeout to be delivered. "Score!" he whooped as he pulled out a couple of frozen pizzas and heated the oven. In thirty minutes they'd have cheesy, meaty goodness to satisfy their hunger.

He grabbed a couple of beers and headed back to the living room to settle down and wait. Within a couple of minutes, Maddox returned and gingerly sat on the couch with a sigh.

Tristan handed him one of the cold beers. "Pizza's cooking, beer's cold, and if you're not hurting too bad..." He dropped to his knees and moved between Maddox's open legs. "I'm hungry for a taste of you."

Maddox bit his lip, "Like I'd tell you no."

"And look at that, you wore some loose shorts to the living room. Easy access for the win." Tristan grabbed the sides and pulled them down until his cock was exposed.

He loved seeing the look of love and lust on his boyfriend's face, especially when he was at his mercy, like he was now. He leaned forward and licked the head as he watched Maddox close his eyes at the feeling. "You taste so good."

"Don't be a cock tease, it's unbecoming of a lover."

Tristan shrugged but decided maybe he was right and he should just get to it. He opened his mouth wide and engulfed Maddox from tip to root.

"Holy fuck," Maddox yelled as he laced his fingers through Tristan's hair to hold on.

Tristan laughed as much as he could with the large cock in his mouth and throat. Maddox let out a needy whine at the sensation. He pulled back as he hollowed his cheeks to give extra suction before going back down. Tristan bobbed his head, alternating with suction, licks, and humming until

Maddox was a quivering mess, pleading for him to make him come.

"You look so hot like this, but I need you to finish me, damn it."

Tristan pulled back until only the head was in his mouth as he ran his tongue over the slit. He stared into Maddox's eyes as he reached under him and tapped at his hole. He knew how sensitive that area could be when he was this close.

"Fuck me," Maddox moaned as he thrust his hips up into Tristan's mouth and came down his throat. "That's it baby, take it all."

Tristan swallowed and then pulled off with a pop, and then leaned up so he could kiss him. "How are you feeling now? Was it too much?"

Maddox shook his head. "Nothing with you will ever be too much."

Tristan smiled as he stood up. "My knees hurt and my stomach is growling. Time to feed my other appetite."

CHAPTER
Twenty-Seven

MADDOX OPENED JEFFREY BARNES'
laptop and scrolled through his search history. He
wasn't a tech guru like Cole, but he was pretty good.
Program by program, he went through everything.
Jeffrey wasn't a fan of an online calendar, so there
was no way to track him that way.

When he opened the mail app, four hundred
emails loaded. All unread and most of them spam.
There were a few emails from the sister writing to
him like he was still around and she was just filling
him in on her day-to-day life.

One of the last opened emails was from a dating
app called 'Mated4Life' saying he had a match.

Maddox frowned as he scrolled back up to the
top and went through the emails one more time.

He opened the first one he came to from 'Mated4Life' and read the message that stated he had new possible connections and to log in to see them.

"Has anybody heard of the 'Mated4Life' dating app?" Maddox asked absently as he clicked the link to take him to the website.

Josh laughed, "Uh, pretty sure that's a supe site, so that leaves me out."

Tristan nodded, "Me too. I went from human to meeting this sexy ass supe who wooed me and claimed my ass."

"I'm pretty sure you are the one who wooed me." Maddox shot back.

Tristan shrugged, "I'll admit I chased your ass, and can you blame me? It's a mighty fine one."

Maddox rolled his eyes as he called out into the pod, "Any of you ever used the dating app Mated4Life?"

Raelle rolled her chair to the door of her office. "It's my main source of finding dates."

Maddox got up and walked over to her. "Can you pull up Jeffrey Barnes? I'm just curious what his profile shows."

She pulled her phone out of her back pocket and opened the app. Maddox whistled as several pop-ups kept them from using the app. "Geez. Do you go on a lot of dates?"

She shrugged. "I have a healthy sex life, if that's what you're asking. I don't go out with all these guys. It all depends on the vibe I get when I'm messaging with them."

When she finally cleared the last message, she typed in the vic's name and it showed three within thirty miles. He pointed to the picture of the one they were looking into. She clicked on the profile and handed Maddox her phone.

He scrolled through. Everything he said about himself was basically what his sister had said. Not that he had expected anything obvious to pop out, but it was still worth looking at.

He handed Raelle her phone back. "Thanks, and be careful out there."

He went back to his office and plopped into his chair. "There is just nothing else on this guy. All the calls back from the bars in the area say the same thing. Jeff went in there a lot, but never seemed to have any trouble with anyone."

Tristan nodded. "I can see why this one went cold. Everybody I talked to had good things to say about him. He loved his life and was happy."

"Hey Maddox," Josh interrupted suddenly, "That

reminds me, did you ever get any hits on the databases on Lopez you were running on Monday?"

He nodded as he logged back into his computer. "The shifter database doesn't show any pings against him other than the agents and police who've been looking into him. I've got facial recognition software running on the four cases we have left. As the results came in, I was going to divvy them up between us. I started with Lopez and I've gotten two hundred and eighty hits where it's a seventy percent or better match. Any free time I have, I've been going through them and eliminating everyone that's not him. I expect results for Vasquez next."

A whistle from the pod area caught their attention. "Yo, come check this out," Derek called out.

Everyone raced into the room and circled around the tv. It was a breaking news alert showing a podium with a scroll below, saying a press conference was about to begin regarding the missing senator.

Maddox pulled up a chair. "This should be interesting."

A man in a suit walked up to the podium and waited for everyone to quiet down. "Good afternoon. I'm Director Daniel Meadows with the Federal

Bureau of Investigation. We can now confirm that Senator Crump was kidnapped. A group called 'The Allied Supernatural Syndicate' have sent in a video with proof that they had taken the senator in retaliation for the murder of the supernatural activist Jasper Pollen and for Senator Crump's bill concerning the tagging of supernaturals. We have received proof of Senator Crump's death and have notified his family. The President has been receiving round-the-clock updates. This group was unknown to us before this. We believe they were recently created in response to escalating tensions over the last year. We urge all Americans, human and paranormal, not to take justice into their own hands. There is no place for vigilantism here. At this time we are not taking any questions. Thank you and have a good day."

The feed cut back to the show that was previously on. The room was silent as everyone processed the news.

Maddox had never heard of the group. The fact that they organized so quickly and were able to easily kidnap a sitting senator scared the hell out of him. These were no novices. These people had to have training.

Kiely had her hand over her mouth. "I am shook

right now. I did not expect him to be killed. This is all seriously fucked up."

Jayden paced the room. "There's no way this is going to end. Each side is just going to keep going at the other."

Tristan's jaw hung open. "Really? No one else is going to say it? Why the hell are paranormals so bad at naming things? First, we're P.I.S. and now these vigilantes are calling themselves A.S.S.?"

Cross broke the tension by laughing loudly. "Holy shit. You're right. That's hysterical."

Vic slammed through the doors. "I'm not sure what the hell is so funny. Have you seen the news?" He waited for people to nod. "We've received word the National Guard is coming in tonight. Since this is the Senator's area, they expect the worst of the fallout to happen here."

"Oh goody," Maddox grumbled. "Can we just say Florida is closed? We've had enough. Stay home."

Ensley flipped through the channels, going between news stations. "I don't think it works that way."

Maddox pushed himself up. "Not that that wasn't exciting news, but I'm going back to staring at facial rec pics. I've only got a couple hundred to go."

He wanted to call his mom and tell her to take

the girls and go to the fae realm for a while, but they'd worked so hard on the wedding he'd hate to mess it up for them. He had to hope the world would keep from burning until after Saturday. He wasn't going to let anyone mess with his mom's special day. She'd waited twenty-five years for her life to start and he would do what he needed to make that happen.

Twenty-Eight

"FINALLY GOT MANCINI'S LAPTOP," Tristan walked into the office and held up the box. "I was starting to think Bertie forgot to send it."

Before he could sit down and open it, Logan walked in and clapped his hands to get everyone's attention. "It's training time. Let's go. I've got uniforms in the lockers for those who need them."

Josh looked up in wide-eyed terror, "Uh, exactly who is going and is it mandatory?"

Tristan laughed as he jumped up to his feet, "Oh, I'm so not missing this."

Logan waved his hand around the pod. "All of you, let's go. You got to learn to work with your team and how to defend against a paranormal."

"Wait, what?" Tristan whined as he dropped

back into his seat. "Who sanctioned this and why are we just hearing about it now for the first time? Last time I trained with you, it didn't end well, remember?"

"That was different." Logan shrugged carelessly. "But you do make a good point. I'll need to check that no one else has any unresolved PTSD issues that I should be warned about."

"I think it was more that a giant fucking bear was suddenly charging me a week after I was attacked and left for dead. Hell, I did die. Cut me a bit of slack, man." Tristan grumbled as Vic walked into the pod and called for everyone's attention.

"I see Logan is here to collect you. I apologize, but with everything that's happened the last few days, I forgot to warn you this was coming up. This came down from the higher-ups, so don't be complaining to me. I can't get you out of it." Vic stared at Tristan as he said the last part with a pointed look. "You all are accomplished officers of the law. You can handle whatever he throws at you. This is only an exercise in building trust amongst you and seeing what you could face in the field."

Josh scowled as he looked at Maddox. "Why does that not make me feel any better in the least?"

Maddox gave him a shit-eating grin. "Maybe

because you know Logan is going to kick all of our asses and not take mercy on you just because you're human?"

Tristan laughed as Josh flicked him off.

"I can't believe I'm saying this, but I think Willow is lucky she got hurt and didn't have to go through this torture." Lexi groaned as she limped back into the pod and dropped into a chair.

"It's not that bad." Ensley laughed as she patted her on the shoulder as she walked by. "You did really good today."

Jaylen laughed, "Are you kidding me? Even my hair hurts."

Tristan walked in whistling, which made all the humans glare at him. "What? It's not like I did this to you. I'm just glad that it's not me dying this time. I've been where you are. I feel your pain."

Vic came out of his office and shook his head at the disheveled group standing around. "Go home, rest up, and be ready for tomorrow. It's going to be another hell of a day."

Tristan raced to his office, excited to be free at a decent hour. His back muscles were finally loose again, so he was hoping he could get Maddox to go flying with him. Now that he'd gotten a taste of the freedom, he couldn't wait to do it again.

"You got hot plans tonight or something?" Josh asked as he came walking in slowly, favoring his left side.

"You never know, I've been talking to this hot cop and tonight might be my lucky night." Tristan waggled his eyebrows.

"To be young and in love." Josh laughed as he grabbed his jacket. "Have fun. My wife is waiting for me with a heating pad and dinner."

Tristan smiled, "I think that's pretty awesome, though. She obviously loves you still. That's pretty damn special."

Josh nodded, "It is. I'm damn lucky and she reminds me of that every day. Don't you doubt that for a minute."

He sat in his chair with a smile as he waited for Maddox to finish whatever he was doing and come find him so they could leave together.

"Are you smiling in your sleep or daydreaming over there?" Maddox asked as he came into the office and set some papers down on his desk.

"I was thinking of you, if you must know." Tristan

stood up and pulled Maddox into his arms. "In case I haven't told you today, I love you."

Maddox smiled and gave him a gentle kiss.

"What do you think about going flying? It's been a couple of days and I really want to do it again. It's still early and then maybe we can get dinner or go to Froggy's and have a drink."

"I've been waiting for you to ask to go flying again. You haven't flown over the city yet. It's incredible and so much better than a gym or over a stadium of crying people."

Tristan laughed, "Can we leave from here and then either come back and get my car or just fly here in the morning?"

Maddox nodded, "Come on, we can take off from the roof."

He wasn't sure he'd ever get tired of this feeling of excitement that he got to fly, and yeah, the fear of jumping off was still there, too. As he stood on the edge, he smiled at Maddox. "You don't have to hold my hand this time. I think I'm ready."

"What if I like holding your hand?"

Tristan held out his hand palm up with a smile, "You don't have to ask. You can take it anytime you want, babe."

Their wings popped out and Tristan shivered as

the breeze fluttered through them and gave him the chills.

"On three?" Maddox asked.

They counted together in unison and then leaped out over the side of the building. Tristan whooped in excitement as they caught a current. Maddox joined in the laughter as he pointed. "Let's go this way. We can go along the coastline and detour inland and when you're ready, circle back here or go home."

"I'll follow you wherever you go, love."

It wasn't just words. Maddox was his home, and he'd follow him wherever he went for as long as the other man wanted him at his side. Maddox had proven that he'd be there for Tristan no matter what came up or how surly and angry he got. Hell, if Maddox hadn't shied away from him when he'd first turned and had been a bit of a jackass, then he was pretty sure nothing would scare him away.

Tristan whooped in laughter as a group of birds flew up beside them for a couple of miles before splitting off and heading out to the water. Maddox was right. This was so much better than flying anywhere else. From up here, he could see people walking and jogging along Bayshore Boulevard, golfers teeing up on the green. Kids outside playing and laughing and enjoying life. None of the strife and turmoil that was currently rocking the city and country. For a minute, he could almost forget about all the shit that was going on.

They banked inland and flew over the highway, their laughter as the speeding cars below rocked the surrounding air filled the sky. Tristan felt like he was on a rollercoaster without a seatbelt. It was exhilarating and scary, and he never wanted it to end.

After a few minutes, Maddox led them off to the side. Tristan smiled his thanks as flying suddenly became easier. He was still building up his muscles, and that had taken a lot out of him.

"Tristan, down and to your left." Maddox pointed with a frown.

Below them, they could see barricades and groups of people blocking the roads. It was peaceful for the moment, but they knew how quickly that could and would change.

"I can't tell what streets those are, I need a closer look so we can report it," Tristan called out as he swooped down closer.

"Be careful," Maddox called as he followed him down, as Tristan knew he would.

He'd barely said the words before things were

being thrown at them and shots were being fired into the air around them.

"Fuck," Tristan called as he careened to the left. "I think they got my wing. It's not working properly. I'm going down."

"Can you make it to the other side and away from these fucking idiots?" Maddox called out in worry.

Tristan grimaced, but nodded as the pain in his wing intensified with each flap of it. He wasn't going to make it far at this rate. He scanned the ground below them for a safe place to land. Someplace without a lot of people milling around and no obvious hatred for their kind. But before he could find a spot, his wing locked up, and he fell from the sky.

"Tristan," Maddox screamed.

He couldn't reply. It was taking all of his concentration to land as gently as he could and, considering he was far from graceful with both wings, he knew this was going to be bad.

CHAPTER
Twenty~Nine

MADDOX DOVE DOWNWARD, trying to catch up to Tristan. As a paranormal, it wasn't likely Tristan would get very hurt, but that heavily depended on what he landed on or hit along the way.

Ten feet from the ground, he got close enough to reach out and grabbed Tristan's hand. Tristan's dead weight ended up being too much to handle that close to the ground. All he'd managed to do was slow him down. He couldn't see what they were about to crash into with it being dark out, but it smelled atrocious.

Maddox smacked against something large and metal as he heard Tristan's shriek off to his left.

There were no hills in Tampa, but somehow they were rolling down a very smelly, very bumpy one.

When they finally came to a stop at the bottom, Maddox was in pain. He'd been jabbed by so many unknown things. When he realized he didn't hear Tristan, he jumped to his feet.

"Babe, where are you?" He listened for a second and honed in on the breathing sound nearby. He grabbed his phone out of his pocket and turned on the flashlight. After a bit of searching, he found Tristan with a large cardboard box on top of him.

Maddox ripped it away and fell to his knees. "Babe. What hurts?"

Tristan groaned, "The question should be what doesn't. My wing is the worst though, and my back."

Maddox swung his phone around to see where they were. "Just our luck. We get shot out of the sky and crash into a landfill."

Tristan gagged. "That explains the smell."

Maddox pulled his GPS up to see where they had landed.

They were too far from the office or their apartment to walk and they'd have to go through some human areas which wouldn't be smart. "So, would you rather I call an Uber or one of our friends for a ride? And do you think you need a hospital?"

Tristan hesitated. "I'll heal, right? That's what we do, so I should be okay... I think." He paused as he tried to stand up. "Shit, I don't know. I can't move my wing at all."

Maddox blew out a breath and dialed the first person he thought of. "Dad, hi. Listen, we were out flying. Tristan was shot and hurt his wing. Can you portal to the address I send you and we'll walk up to the entrance and meet you? We need you to portal us to Shifter General so he can get checked out."

"It's never a dull moment with this family, is it? Are you okay?" Maddox appreciated Silas thought to ask about him.

"I think I'm okay. I'll take stock of myself when we get to the hospital. Oh and be warned, we stink to high hell."

Silas chuckled, "I'm sure it's not that bad. Send me the address and I'll be waiting for you."

Maddox texted the number and then leaned over Tristan. "We need to walk a bit. It'll take Silas too long to find us out here. I'm going to pick you up, so hang on."

Before Tristan could protest, Maddox scooped him up. "I can walk, there is no way in Hell I'm letting your dad see me carried out of here like this."

Maddox didn't want to set him down. He was

worried about him and wanted to help, but he understood Tristan's not wanting to be seen that way. He kept his arm around Tristan's shoulders as he lowered his feet and held on while he got his footing.

Tristan gasped. "Shit. My wing just tried to go inside me, but it can't. I think they really fucked it up."

"Don't focus on that right now. Let's worry about getting to the front and then the doctors can tell us what's what."

They walked in pained silence for several minutes. The sounds of flapping wings and birds fighting caught their attention. Maddox steered them toward the sound.

"I know we're in a dump, but vultures don't usually care about discarded food and trash... right?"

"Nope, and that's what's got me curious. I won't drag you far. If we don't see anything, we'll just keep heading toward my dad."

They skirted around another hill of garbage and were assailed by an odor they knew all too well. "You smell that?"

"I wish I could say no, but it's too distinctive to be anything else."

"I've never seen so many vultures in one spot." It looked like hundreds were scattered across the field in front of them. Whatever they were picking at had them in a frenzy. "Can you handle getting a little closer, or do you want me to leave you here for a second and go see what's up?"

"We're in this together. Let's go."

They hobbled the rest of the way around the trash pile. Maddox whistled and waved his one free arm around, scaring the birds closest to them. "Hang on, I need to bend down." He waited until Tristan was steady before letting go and squatting down.

His flashlight scanned the disturbed ground and froze when he saw a hand sticking up out of the dirt. "Fuck me." He stood back up. "Change of plans. Let me get the team down here, and then I'll get you to the hospital."

He hit the button to call Vic, who answered on the second ring. "I hope you're just calling to wish me a good night."

"If only. Very long story short, Tristan and I are at a landfill and there's a body. Based on the number of vultures, I'm guessing there's more than one. Tristan is hurt though, so I need someone here asap to take over the scene while we go to the hospital."

Vic cursed. "Only you two... How bad is he?"

Maddox hesitated, "I don't know. He was shot and his wing isn't working."

"I'll alert the team. Sheppard and Kiely can get there faster. Leave as soon as one of them gets there." Vic blew out a breath. "And keep me in the loop about his condition."

"Okay. Tell Kiely we were shot down, so she needs to avoid human areas. Oh, and my dad is at the front gate waiting to portal us. Can one of them grab him on their way in?"

"Not a problem. What's the name of the place?"

"Covington Waste Management."

"Got it. We'll be there soon."

Maddox slid his phone back into his pocket. "Okay. Now we get to see who's faster, the vampire or the pegasus."

It was only a few minutes before Sheppard skidded to a stop in front of them. "You two look like hell and I barely managed to find you because your scents are so well hidden by all the rot. It's impressive that you smell as bad as rotting corpses and garbage."

"I guess the vampire was faster." Tristan groaned as he tried to make a joke.

Sheppard shook his head. "We arrived about the same time, but your dad felt more comfortable flying than being carried by me." He pointed above them. "Here they are now."

Silas looked like a regal King as he was brought down by the pegasus. He immediately slid off Kiely and ran over to them. "You can catch the team up later. Let's get you guys out of here."

He wrapped his arm around Tristan's other side and opened a portal. They stepped through and were immediately at the entrance of the emergency room. The staff didn't look surprised to see people walk through a portal, but they recognized they were injured and jumped into action.

Tristan was laid on his side on a gurney and rushed away. Maddox tried shooing the nurses away.

"Enough," Silas demanded. "We are here. Get yourself checked out. You have nothing but time while Tristan is being looked at."

Maddox had never heard such authority in his dad's voice before. "Yes, sir."

He growled when the nurse tried to make him get in a wheelchair. "Just point the way. I can walk."

As he was led through a curtained area, he texted Obinski to let him know they were there.

The doctor responded almost immediately that he'd be there in fifteen minutes. It really was nice having a doctor on speed dial. Even if part of him felt bad that he was coming back in after having spent most of the last two days with his family and coworkers.

A young nurse walked in, smiling at him. "I hear we have a grumpy patient. Don't worry, I got you the hospital gown with clowns on it to cheer you up."

"Fuck me," Maddox growled.

CHAPTER
Thirty

TRISTAN YAWNED as he was wheeled out of the hospital with Maddox walking beside him, scowling at everyone they passed. "Did they give you an enema or something? You look like you're going to kill someone."

Silas snickered as he met up with them, "They wouldn't let him sit with you until he was checked out and cleaned up. Plus, he was being an ass, so they might have gotten a bit of revenge." Silas winked at Tristan as he pulled out his phone. "Don't worry, I got pictures for you. The girls and Marta are going crazy over it."

Maddox groaned as he glared at his father. "You didn't?"

Silas shrugged. "I couldn't help it. You looked so adorable."

"Can't even trust my own father."

Tristan laughed. It was times like this he realized just how much he'd missed out on with his own father.

"Marta wants you both to call her when you have a minute. She's worried sick about you boys. I told her you were okay, but she won't listen until she sees for herself." Silas gave both of them a pointed look that dared them to argue with him. "Now, what do you want to do from here? Do I take you home, to the office, or back to the dump?" He looked them both up and down and cringed. "I'd suggest you go home and take a shower, but that's just my opinion since I'm standing so close to you both."

Maddox rolled his eyes at his father. "Vic ordered us home to get cleaned up. If the doctors gave us an all-clear, he'd allow us back at the office in the morning."

Tristan laughed. "That's putting it nicely. But going home to a hot shower and a couple of hours of sleep would be pretty fantastic right now."

Silas nodded, "Then let's get you home, and don't be surprised if you're woken up early with a call from Marta. It took everything I had to get her to stay home with the girls when she heard you'd been shot."

Tristan smiled, "I look forward to it, honestly. It's been a long time since I had a mother to worry about me like that."

"Babe, you're part of our family, so get used to them all worrying about you." Maddox winked as he helped Tristan stand. "Now let's go home. We've got a long day ahead of us."

The ringing of his phone woke him the next morning. He groaned as he tried to roll over and yelped as his back protested the position. "Shit balls, I didn't think that one through." He muttered as he reached for the offending object that had started this hell off.

"Hello."

"I gave you as long as I could. Now we need you at the office to get your statements," Vic announced abruptly.

Tristan groaned as he looked around and noticed Maddox wasn't in bed anymore. "What the hell time is it?"

Vic sighed. "Just after eight. Your boyfriend isn't

answering his phone. Find him and get in here as soon as you can. This is going to be all hands on deck with what you discovered last night."

"Fine." Tristan grunted as he hit end on the call and let it drop on the bed beside him. He climbed out of the bed and went in search of Maddox. He followed the soft murmurs to the living room, where he found him on a video call with his family.

"Mom, he's awake." Maddox grinned as he passed him the phone. "I'll go get dressed while you reassure her you're okay."

Tristan smiled at the phone as he sat down, "Hey Marta."

"Tristan, we've been so worried about you."

"I'm fine, I promise," Tristan reassured her. "A little banged up, but nothing that won't heal pretty quick. I already feel much better."

Marta sighed, "Fine, but I expect you boys here for dinner in the next day or so. I need to see for myself you're okay."

Tristan agreed, said goodbye, and hung up. Then he stood up and went to chase Maddox down again.

"Maddox?" He called out as he entered their bedroom. "Everything okay?"

"Yeah, my phone wouldn't stop and it woke me

up. I saw some messages from Vic. I take it we're needed?"

"Yeah, it's all hands on deck," he said. "Apparently, it's a bigger mess than we realized last night."

Maddox groaned, "You get dressed and I'll start the coffee. Hell, I might even need some after last night."

An hour later, they were walking into their pod, which was a flurry of activity. Vic noticed them first. "I'm sorry I had to do this. First things first, how are you feeling? I know they cleared you, but nothing more than that."

Tristan nodded. "The bullet hit a muscle in my wing, which caused it to go numb and freeze up. It's already healing, though. They said there won't be any lasting damage."

"Good," Vic turned to Maddox, "and you?"

"Just some scrapes, bruises, and a few shallow cuts. I'm good to go." Maddox glanced around, "Fill us in on what's happened."

"It's a fucking mess. You boys stumbled onto one hell of a body dump." Vic motioned for them to follow him to the whiteboard they'd set up. "We've got the forensics tech's out there collecting what they can, but as you can imagine, it's not going to be much besides the actual bodies and parts."

Tristan grimaced, "Wait, did you say parts?"

Vic nodded. "Yes, they're bringing them in as they are done being processed. We've set up the gym as a temporary staging area. TPD tried taking over, but one of the skulls was very obviously a troll and not human."

Maddox rubbed his temples. "Any idea how many bodies there are?"

Vic was handed a note by an agent. He scanned it before answering. "When I left, they were thinking there were at least ten different bodies there. But that was just by sight. I think when they do the DNA testing, it will be a much higher count."

Ensley walked in and shrieked when she saw them. "Dudes. You guys are so lucky. That dump is insane. I mean, we didn't need the extra work or anything, but still... awesome find."

Tristan shook his head. "You scare me."

Kiely walked in a second later. Maddox walked over. "Thank you for getting there so fast last night and giving my dad a ride. I know that can be awkward."

She shrugged him off. "Please. Your dad is hot. If he wasn't marrying your mom, I would say he could ride me anytime, but..."

Vic groaned. "I'm right here guys. Have some decency. We're in the office."

Everyone looked at him and burst into laughter. "Insubordinate, the whole lot of you."

"And you wouldn't want us any other way." Tristan gave him a cheeky smile.

"Hmmm, I'm not so sure about that. Now go get your reports written up and then check in at the gym. Johnson was in charge last time I was down there. I'm sure he would love your help."

"Oh, hell no. Come on Vic, send us to the dump. I still haven't gotten the smell of rot out of my hair. I'll help dig up body parts. Just don't make me deal with Bruce." Maddox begged.

"All of you are crazy. He's a peach." Ensley interjected.

"Let me guess, you guys bonded over a body?" Tristan shot back.

"His knowledge of the more obscure ways to kill a person is truly impressive. We're in an online chat group that meets twice a month. He's very friendly to everyone in there."

Tristan's jaw fell open. "We can't be talking about the same person."

Vic smacked a folder on the table. "Enough. We have more work than we know what to do with. You two get to your statements and the rest of you are either working on the dump case or your missing people."

"Yes, dad," Tristan mumbled as he rushed to his office.

It took them over an hour to write up their statements. They turned them in and then, with trepidation, headed to the gym to check in with Bruce.

"This isn't going to go over well at all," Tristan mumbled as he pulled open the gym doors and froze at the overwhelming smell that had already filled the large space.

Maddox stepped back in shock and then straightened his spine and looked around for the tech. "There he is."

They worked their way around the outside of the large square they'd set up until they could call out to Bruce. He scowled at them before marching over with narrowed eyes. "What the hell are you two doing down here?"

"Vic said to see if you needed any help with anything." Tristan hedged.

Bruce rolled his eyes. "Neither of you is qualified. Get your asses out of my lab. If and when we find something you can help with, we'll let you know. In the meantime, you're just in my way."

Tristan saluted the asshole, turned on his heel, and headed back to their office. He had enough shit to do without listening to that jackass anyway. Maybe he'd finally get a minute to look into the Mancini laptop.

CHAPTER
Thirty~One

MADDOX FELT like his eyes were crossing. He'd already managed to remove a hundred and twenty potential pics of Raul Lopez and he felt like the list was never-ending. At least the Maria Vasquez potential photos came back, so Josh was in misery with Maddox as he scrolled through each image.

"I got into Mancini's Instagram account. Lucky us, he'd left his login credentials. His agent was right about how popular he was. He's got a couple hundred thousand followers. His DMs are full of solicitations, job offers, and requests for meetings with new agents. It looks like he ignored most of them, but for some reason, he'd been conversing with a Kyle Masters about a photo shoot."

Maddox looked over Tristan's shoulder and

glanced at the DMs. "Damn, there are a lot of horny people out there. They seriously treated him like a piece of meat."

"As a twenty-four-year-old, he probably loved the attention," Josh said over his shoulder.

"We need to check with Bertie and see if he knows anything about this." Tristan tapped his fingers on the desk. "It looks like they'd set up a date for a photo shoot, but it doesn't say when or where. They switched to phone calls. The last Instagram post was dated the day before Bertie said he texted Antonio about the shoot he'd set up." He turned the laptop around so they could see the picture. "This is the last pic he posted, and it says #newopportunities #bigtime #photoshoot #luckytobechosen #newadventure #differentpath."

Maddox whistled. "Damn, when I went to the gym, the guys never looked like that. Now I wish I had never stopped going."

"Wow, way to make a guy feel inferior," Tristan grumbled as he turned the laptop back around. "Fucking gym rats."

Maddox put his hand on top of Tristan's head and made him tilt back to look up at him. "We can admire anyone as long as it's just a look and we go home to each other, right?"

Tristan shrugged, "Yeah, I guess. Doesn't mean I like hearing about you talking like you want something different, but yeah, as long as you come home to me, we're good."

"I'm sorry. We both know you have a weird obsession with the guy from the pizza commercials, and I don't have a problem with it."

"Pizza guy?" Josh questioned.

"Um…" Tristan laughed sheepishly, "He's got this whole cute, wholesome twink vibe and he's holding a really big meat lover's pizza. It's like a fantasy come true."

Josh held his hands up. "I can't judge. That lady from the insurance commercials with her little apron and fifties hair bob does something to me, too."

Tristan bit his lip to keep from laughing as he looked up at Maddox in wide-eyed wonder.

"Straight people," Maddox whispered.

"So… uh… back to the Instagram thing. It could be nothing, but I think I'm going to run a check on this Kyle guy and see what pops up. It's not adding up he'd talk to another agent when Bertie had him set up with a huge print ad that was going to put him on the map."

Maddox went back to flipping through pictures.

267

This was the tedious part of the job no one ever wanted to talk about.

At picture two hundred and eleven, he got excited. He clicked on the image, which took him to the camera feed it was pulled from. It was a security camera at Pier 54 in Seattle. The man was holding hands with a woman and had a small boy on his shoulders. That was definitely not Raul Lopez's wife.

"Hey, someone come look at this. Does this look like Raul to you?"

Josh and Tristan pushed their chairs across the tiny office. They watched the video on repeat a couple of times.

Josh smirked. "I'd bet money that is Raul with a new family."

Maddox glared at the image of the man. "That would be a really shitty thing to do if so." He really wished it wasn't Raul. The last thing he wanted to do was tell the wife here that he'd left her for another family. "I'll call the Seattle office and see if they can run this down for us."

As he made the phone call, Tristan updated the whiteboard to show Raul possibly alive in Seattle.

Maddox's cell buzzed in his pocket. A breaking news alert popped up. "Pull up the news. They have a break on the activist case."

He pulled the news station up on his computer and loaded the live stream. The anchor was filling time waiting for a press conference to start. After a minute, the Chief of Tampa Police stepped up to the microphone. "Good afternoon. I'm Chief Henry Barlowe. I'm very proud of the work my department has done on the shooting case of Jasper Pollen. Late last night, we apprehended the gunman responsible for the assassination." A mugshot came up of a white man in his forties. "The assailant is forty-three-year-old Max Hart. We received information that the human supremacy group 'The Chosen Ones' has claimed responsibility for the shooting. We have an extensive history with this group and have a long list of known members. During the investigation, a single shell casing with a partial fingerprint was recovered. We were able to match that to Mr Hart. This is the fourth major incident in the last two weeks. We want to echo the words of the F.B.I. Director and remind everyone there is no place in Tampa Bay for vigilantism. There will be no more questions."

Maddox closed the live stream. "I hate those Chosen One's mother fuckers. I've had run-ins with them before and they are real pieces of shit. I'm not surprised at all they did this."

Josh rolled his chair around to face them. "I've arrested a few in my time with TPD, too. This seems a little high profile for them, but maybe they are escalating."

Maddox grabbed his phone. "You know what? I need a freaking drink. I'm texting everyone and telling them the first round is on me for finding that dump site and causing them all a lot of extra work."

He typed up the message and hit send. A second later, Josh's and Tristan's phones buzzed. "Obviously you guys are invited, but figured I'd formally invite you."

Tristan logged off his computer and grabbed his keys. "Works for me. I have some searches running on the Kyle guy, so maybe tomorrow I'll have results."

Maddox followed suit and went out to the pod. Vic was still standing near the whiteboard. He had stress lines around his eyes. "Did you get my text about getting a drink?"

Vic nodded. "Sure did, but I'll have to pass. I have a lot to do here and I've been up all night, so I'm going to crash early."

"Sounds good. Don't work too late."

The rest of the team made their way out of their

offices, making jokes about how many rounds the case was really worth.

For all the shit they go through and the bad things they see, he was grateful they still had their sense of humor and were able to disconnect and unwind. Otherwise, they all might end up as crazy as Ensley.

CHAPTER
Thirty~Two

TRISTAN GRABBED the beers off the bar and headed to the tables they'd pushed together. He handed Maddox one of the glasses and sat next to him. "I was just thinking since we're sitting here we could see if Ceka wants to come here and meet up with Sicily and Mick. They can interview her away from us, but we'll be here in case anything goes down."

Maddox pulled out the secure phone from his back pocket. "Look at you having good ideas. It's short notice, but maybe, being a Thursday night, they'll all be available. Ceka's phone is unprotected, so I'll have to word it carefully and hope she comes."

Tristan sipped his beer while Maddox sent the coded messages.

Finneas walked in to several cheers. It was amazing how quickly he had won over everyone. Logan came in just after him and pulled out the chair next to Tristan for Finneas, then he sat next to him.

Tristan leaned over to Maddox. "Is it just me, or does Logan seem a little dazzled by our new fae friend?"

Maddox glanced up from his phone and shrugged. "Maybe he was just being nice."

"Ugh, men. Sometimes we're so oblivious."

Maddox slid his phone back into his pocket. "I think all our friends are coming for a drink."

Froggy walked up and slapped Maddox on the back. "I heard you are buying ten rounds for everyone tonight."

"What!" Maddox glared at them. "I said one and let's avoid top-shelf."

Kiely held her hand over her heart. "Ugh, not even worth the best? I let your dad ride me."

Froggy lifted one eyebrow. "Okay, now I really want the story."

"Let?" Tristan asked with a laugh. "I heard you say if he wasn't engaged you'd go after him."

Kiely shrugged, "I'm equal opportunity... as long as both parties are single, that is."

Jaylen walked up with a smile. "I love this song, it always makes me want to dance."

Finneas turned and smiled. "I don't think we've been properly introduced, but if you don't mind dancing with a guy. I'd be happy to take a turn with you."

Logan turned to Tristan and whispered, "A turn with you?"

Tristan laughed. "I think he's saying he'll dance with him. Get your mind out of the gutter."

"I'm Jaylen and I'd love to." He said as he held out his hand to Finneas. "I love to dance."

"Hey babe, how come you never dance with me?" Tristan whined to Maddox. "Look how cute they are out there."

"You call that cute?" Logan demanded incredulously. "Look at the human, he's flopping around like a dying fish."

"He looks like he's having more fun than you are," Jasmina teased.

Maddox tugged at Tristan's arm. "You know my issues with having people look at me. If dancing is that important to you, I will get up right now and shake it for everyone to see."

Tristan smiled as he leaned in and kissed

Maddox. "That you offered is enough for me. But I will let you get me another drink."

Maddox turned and waved at Froggy. "Another round for Tristan and it's okay if it's top-shelf."

A chorus of boos had him laughing. They were so easy to get a rise out of.

"Hey, should we put a limit on you two tonight?" Reed asked with a straight face. "You did have to be bailed out of jail a few days ago. We have reputations to uphold, you know."

Tristan flicked him off with a laugh, "I got hurt, I need the comfort, you ass."

A few minutes later, Maddox nudged him and gestured to the door where he saw Sicily entering. She gave him a nod and then moved to an empty booth on the other side of the room. Within five minutes, Mick had arrived as well. Now they were just waiting on Ceka. As the minutes ticked by, he grew more anxious that something had happened.

"Have you heard anything?" Tristan asked Maddox. "Shouldn't she be here by now?"

Maddox nodded, but before he could reply, the door opened, and Ceka entered. She stood frozen in the doorway in wide-eyed terror. Tristan jumped up and raced over to her with a smile.

"Hey, is everything okay?"

"Yes, I was just nervous. Is it safe to come in? I left my phone behind like you instructed." Ceka took in the room. "There's a lot of people here."

Tristan nodded. "But most of them are on our side. They are part of my team, helping us to figure this out and reunite you with your family." He turned and pointed to the booth where Sicily and Mick sat. "Those are the people we told you about. They are going to help, but they need you to tell them your story. We'll be right here the whole time and if you need us, we'll come get you. You're safe here, I promise."

Ceka nodded as slowly walked over to the two reporters and sat down.

Tristan blew out a breath of relief as he headed back to Maddox and the rest of the team. He wasn't sure if this was going to help or not, but they figured the more the reporters knew, the better the chances they'd be able to help or at least expose what was happening when the time came.

"Who's up for a game of pool or darts?" Sheppard called out to the table.

"I haven't played darts in years. I'm in." Derek jumped up and two of them headed off, with Lexi and Ensley following behind, heckling them.

Tristan laughed as he heard some of the creative

comments coming out of their mouths. "Hey, Logan. You up for a game of pool?"

Logan frowned and shook his head. "Nah, maybe later though."

"Sure." Tristan grinned as he moved to sit next to Cross. "Help me out here."

Cross gave him a questioning look. "What can I help you with exactly? And remember, your boyfriend is my friend."

"Wow, damn." Tristan laughed, "What exactly do you think I'm going to ask of you?"

Cross shrugged. "Just putting it out there, just in case."

Tristan pointed to Logan and then Finneas. "Maddox doesn't see it, but I can't be the only one who's noticed the attention Logan is giving to Finneas. You've seen it, right?"

Cross stared at Logan and then turned to watch Finneas. "I don't know, maybe. They're friends and work out a lot together, so maybe that's what you're seeing. I don't know Finneas well, but I do know that he's a huge flirt."

"Babe, stop." Maddox muttered as he placed a drink in front of him. "Let them figure it out. Come play pool with me."

"The last time we played pool, we ended up arrested. Are you sure it's a good idea?"

Cross jumped with a laugh. "Oh, I'm coming to watch this for sure." He turned and called to Reed, "Hey, come on, you don't want to miss this."

"What's wrong with him?" Tristan leaned in and whispered so that Reed wouldn't hear over the loud music.

"His wife is nagging him to come home. She's not happy about the long hours that are going to be coming up dealing with the bodies. She's been pushing him to quit the agency, if you can believe that bullshit. He'll be miserable. He loves this job." Cross shook his head in frustration as he followed Tristan and Maddox to the pool table. "So what's the bet?"

Maddox sighed, "No bets. I promised Vic we'd behave and make sure everyone made it to work tomorrow without any issues."

Tristan laughed as he heard the team boo him and his rules. When he'd worked for the TPD, he'd had friends and hung out with the other cops, but never had he had this sense of family like he did with this group. Getting turned was the best thing that could ever have happened to him.

CHAPTER
Thirty-Three

"YOU LOOK like you had a good time last night. You must have had a hot date." Maddox laughed as Tristan stumbled into the kitchen bleary-eyed.

Tristan grunted as he reached for the coffee cup on the counter and sighed with his first sip.

Maddox chuckled at the absolute peace on Tristan's face that one sip had given him. "You're as obsessed with coffee as Ensley is with serial killers."

"This is a good, safe obsession, one that millions agree with me on."

"I'll give you that. And as long as it makes you happy, I'll continue to get it for you." He kissed the side of Tristan's head and went to put on his shoes. "Finish your coffee and get dressed. We have the pod meeting today and a lot to do before the rehearsal dinner tonight."

Tristan gulped the rest of the coffee and shuffled back toward the bedroom. "I am really looking forward to tonight. There has been so much shit going on. It's nice to be celebrating something."

Maddox couldn't agree more. Now that he'd come to terms with his parent's relationship, he couldn't wait for them to tie the knot and start their new life.

Tristan nursed his second cup of coffee as they drove into the office. They filed into the pod at the same time as everyone else.

Vic took one look around the room and snorted. "You all look a little worse for wear, but everyone showed up and that's what counts. Everyone get settled. We have a lot to go over today."

He waited while everyone collected their notes from their offices and sat down. "As for the dump case, they think they have at least fifteen unique bodies, but until testing comes back, they can't confirm. I stopped by the dump on my way in and I think the number is going to be higher than that. They've started running tests on the parts as they come in and the lab is treating them as the highest priority so I assume we'll start getting some results later today."

Maddox blinked in surprise. When he had seen the hand sticking up, he knew there was a body, but he hadn't been expecting them to find multiple bodies.

Vic tossed his notepad down on the table. "Maddox, Tristan, and Josh, you guys go first."

Maddox cleared his throat. "We have definitely cleared one case. The woman won the lottery and took off to Italy."

Jasmina whistled. "Damn. She's living the dream."

Murmurs of agreement went around the room.

"I believe one of our guys is in Seattle living under a different identity and possibly with a whole new family. I have the field office out there running him down."

He glanced at Tristan to continue. "Maria Vasquez was catfished by a couple hiring her to babysit. The couple doesn't exist and so far, we have zero leads. Antonio Mancini was about to do a big photo shoot that was going to change his career. The day before he disappeared. The only thing we have to look into right now is an Instagram Dm where he was talking with a Kyle Masters about a photo shoot.

My preliminary searches didn't find anything with that name and the account was closed. Our last case is Jeffrey Barnes. We have no leads other than a dating app called Mated4Life and a date he had planned for the night he disappeared. We're still looking into him."

Cole tapped his pen on the table. "Two of our cases are complete dead ends, except for similar contacts with someone who no longer exists. Carly Johnson was selling some stuff on Craig's List and was supposed to meet with a buyer on the day of her disappearance. Landon Young was on a single's meet-up forum."

"How is that different from a dating site?" Kiely asked.

Cole shrugged. "From what I understand, the forum is more for finding friends to do activities with you that you both enjoy. He was on there looking for people to go deep sea diving with since he was a shark shifter and could go deeper and faster than an average diver."

Jaylen raised his hand. "The case I'm looking into has zero leads except for an email from a woman inviting him to meet her to sell some of his feathers for her art collection. I haven't been able to track the woman down yet."

The ripple of awareness went around the room at the same time. Vic smiled. "Let's go through the rest of the updates. Then I want everyone to look closer at the cases you still have open and see if the victim was talking with someone new in their life right before their disappearance and then confirm if that person really exists. We may have just found a link between some of our cases."

Thirty minutes later, the meeting was over and there was a buzz of excitement that always came when there was a potential breakthrough.

Tristan went back to his search for the Kyle person while Maddox and Josh scanned potential pictures of Maria.

Two hours later, Maddox leaned back and stretched his back. "I'm calling it. Let's get some lunch. We're overdue for a visit to Mrs Diaz."

Josh smiled brightly. "I was telling my wife how good the food was. I really wish humans could go there. I promised her that next time we went, I'd bring home some food for her to try."

Vic knocked on their door frame. "Got a hit back on one of the parts. It belongs to Jeffrey Barnes. He's one of yours, right?"

"Shit." Tristan cursed. "I was hoping for his sister's sake we'd find him alive somewhere."

"From what I understand, it's only one piece so far, but I'll assign your name to the case, so updates are sent to you as they get them."

Maddox frowned. "That really sucks, but what are the odds we found the field where his body was dumped and there are other bodies and we have other missing people. I have a bad feeling we have a serial killer and we found his disposal site."

When he saw Tallie and Quinn later, he was going to have a long talk with them about talking to strangers online and what to do and not do before they meet someone in real life. They may not be his biological sisters, but he still cared for them like they were and he'd do anything to protect them.

Thirty~Four

TRISTAN PUSHED his chair back from his desk and stood up. "I'm grabbing a coffee. Anyone want anything?"

"I'll take one if you don't mind," Josh called out to his retreating back.

Tristan raised a hand that he'd heard him and headed to the break room. He was beyond frustrated and not sure what to do at this point. He was hitting one dead end after another. They'd established Mancini's prospective agent didn't exist, and from what he could tell, that was the only new person he'd talked to before he'd disappeared.

Barnes' laptop wasn't much better. The only app he couldn't get into was the dating one. The rest had turned up nothing important. The guy was either dead or at least missing a hand. Everything in him told him that the dating app was the key to his disappearance, he just had to find a way to prove it. And right now, he didn't have enough to get a warrant to get access from the company.

Cole grabbed a mug. "What's got your panties in a twist?"

"Red tape and people who don't save their login information on their computers to make it easy for us to get on their sites," Tristan grumbled as he poured coffee into his cup. "I mean, can't something go easy on this damn case?"

"We do spend a lot of time and money trying to educate people not to do that very thing because of hackers." Cole shrugged and turned to face Tristan, "But luckily for you, I'm one of the good guy hackers. Why don't you let me see what I can do to get you in there?"

Tristan hesitated. "Aren't you overwhelmed with your cases and pulling stuff from everyone else? I don't want to overload you or anything."

Cole blew a raspberry. "Dude, I wouldn't offer if I couldn't handle it. Most of those sites' security is shit anyway. It'll take me less time to get in than it would for you to finish that cup of coffee."

"In that case, I'd be stupid to pass this opportunity up and my mother didn't raise a fool." Tristan spun around and raced out of the kitchen and skidded to a halt at his desk.

Josh reached for his drink and frowned. "Hey, what happened to the coffee?"

"Got sidetracked. I'll go back for it in a minute." Tristan grabbed the laptop and headed back, calling out Cole's name as he went.

"Dude, chill, I'm right here. I didn't abandon my coffee, like some weird ass people." Cole held up his mug in a mocking salute. "Give me that, you go get your drinks and I'll let you know when I'm done."

Tristan shrugged one shoulder as he laughed. "I got excited."

He watched Cole walk back into his office before he made his way back to the half-full cups he'd been preparing. If luck was on their side, they'd get some answers about Jeffrey Barnes and tie him in with the rest of the missing supes. They were getting close. He could feel it.

He'd just returned to the office when Maddox's secret phone pinged with a message. Maddox pulled it out of his pocket with a scowl as he looked up at Tristan and Josh.

"Why do I get the feeling this isn't going to be good news?"

He set the phone down on the desk so all three could see it at the same time.

'Another one opened in Albuquerque, all taken.'

"Fucking hell," Tristan snarled as he began to pace.

Vic entered the office with a frown as he flashed his own secret phone at them. "Development down in the gym." Then he turned and walked out.

They laid their phones on their desks and then followed him out and down to the lockers where the rest of the team was assembling. Once they were all there, Vic turned on the showers. "We just got word of another rift that opened in New Mexico. Everyone was taken this time. Somehow, these assholes are ahead of the game and know where they are going to open before they do."

Cole moved around until he was in front of the group. "I've been talking to some 'friends' about what type of technology and equipment would be needed to detect them."

"And what did they come up with?" Cross asked into the silence.

"Basically, it's a technology that doesn't exist yet, at least that we know of. Whoever is hunting these people has the money and the scientists to create it."

Maddox blew out a breath. "Awesome. So we're

up against some seriously shady group that is hacking our federal systems and developed brand new tech to hunt people."

Vic nodded his agreement. "There can't be that many people with these kinds of resources. We should pass this on to the reporters so they can look into it through their channels as well." He turned and shut off the water. "Check in with Sabrina before you head back upstairs. If she needs anything, please help out."

They filed out slowly, each lost in their thoughts as they waited their turn to check in with the ME. After five minutes, Maddox gestured for them to head back upstairs and Tristan was happy to escape back to the case they could actually do something about.

He tried not to watch the clock as the hours ticked by, but he was failing miserably. Josh and Maddox had taken to calling him out on it.

"I'm just saying he said it would take less time than it took me to drink my coffee. I don't know many people that take three hours to drink one cup," Tristan grumbled as he craned his neck to look out into the pod.

Maddox rolled his eyes. "Babe, he has his own

cases he's working too. Maybe something came up, and he had to put your laptop on hold."

Tristan frowned but nodded, "I know. It's just that I know we're gonna find out he's connected to some stranger too and it's just proof that our theory is right. But what's really bugging me is why? Why these people? What happened to them? And why did it happen?"

Josh laughed, "Uh, I hate to break it to you, but that's the same question I have on every case. That's why we're in this job, to figure that shit out."

Maddox pushed his chair back and stood up with a stretch. "It'll all be here Monday, and from what Sabrina said, she'll be working around the clock all weekend. We should know something early next week."

"Who is Sabrina again? I haven't met everybody yet." Josh raised his hand to interrupt.

"Dr Sabrina Jeffries is our ME. She's pretty awesome. You'll love her." Tristan replied as he stood up and grabbed his keys.

"That's right, you have the rehearsal dinner tonight, don't you?" Josh smiled. "That should be fun. You guys have a good time and forget about this place for a little while. It'll be here next week."

"Yeah, tell that to the paranormal that goes

missing this weekend," Tristan growled in frustration as he walked out of the office.

He felt bad for the comment as soon as he said it, he knew logically it wasn't Josh's fault and he'd just been trying to be nice. Tristan was just on edge. Now that they'd found the killing grounds, he worried the asshole would disappear or change things up and they'd have to start over. It'd happened before, after all.

CHAPTER
Thirty-Five

MADDOX YANKED on the tie suffocating him for the hundredth time since leaving the house. He hated when he had to wear a suit. He'd like to say it was because it made him feel restricted, but deep inside, he knew the truth. He hated wearing suits because he always felt like he was too large to look good in them.

Tristan reached across the front seat of the car and grabbed Maddox's hand. "Penny for your thoughts?"

Maddox stared straight ahead rather than look into Tristan's eyes. "Nothing major. A dash of self-loathing, and a pinch of self-consciousness."

Tristan huffed and turned slightly so he could see Maddox better. "I wish you could see what I see when I look at you. You are so fucking gorgeous it kills me. I question why you're with me all the time. The only thing I can think of is that in some past life, I must have done something amazing and you're my reward."

"I really have come a long way since dating you. I always had confidence in my skills but never really thought I was that good looking. Every morning I practice seeing myself through your eyes. It's helping. I have a lot of years to erase, though."

"I'll remind you every day until you believe it."

They pulled into the parking lot of the gardens where the wedding was going to start in less than two hours.

Maddox grabbed his tux bag out of the trunk. "I'm just glad we're not on the bride's side. They've been up for hours getting their hair and makeup done and who knows what else. I'm following Tallie's Snapchat and she looks like she's having a blast though."

Tristan held up his phone, showing Tallie's pics. "I've been watching too. I'm still worried about Quinn having another episode. That poor girl doesn't need any extra attention on her."

Maddox swung open the gates to the building they'd be waiting in before the ceremony started.

"We've been able to keep her name out of the Press so far, but I worry it will come out some day. Let's hope we can get her at full strength before that happens."

"We need to get her started on self-defense and shit soon. I already talked to Logan. He said he would help too."

Maddox pulled Tristan to a stop. "You're a great big brother, you know that? I bet you would make a great father too." He kissed his boyfriend on the mouth and left him standing there.

Mentioning fatherhood probably just blew Tristan's mind, but it's something Maddox had been thinking about lately. He was ready to settle down. He wanted to marry Tristan, buy a big house with a nice backyard, and raise a family with him.

They knocked on the door labeled 'Groom' and went in. Silas stood at a mirror looking at himself in the tux.

Tristan wolf-whistled. "Damn, sir. You really do look amazing."

Maddox raised an eyebrow at him but didn't say anything. He knew Tristan would never stray.

"Thank you, Tristan. I'm sure you both will look just as good." Silas smiled at them in the mirror. "I've heard so much giggling through the walls. It's nice to know the girls are having such a good time. Your mother, and well, all of them deserve it."

"I just wish I had gotten my head out of my ass-" he turned and scowled at Tristan "-don't say a word, got my head out of my ass sooner and made sure mom was happy. I'm sorry if it was my fault you guys had so many years apart."

Silas cupped Maddox's face. "Don't give it another thought. We're together as a family now."

A young woman knocked and entered. "We'll be ready for you to get in place in thirty minutes."

"Thank you, Stacy." Silas nodded and went back to checking himself in the mirror. That was hilarious, considering the man could wear a garbage bag and still look like a runway model.

Tristan poured them each a glass of champagne and passed out the glasses. "May our hearts always be overflowing with love and laughter, our bed never empty and may each day be better than the last."

Maddox pulled him close and kissed him deeply. God, he loved this man.

They finished getting ready and followed Stacy out to the garden. The gazebo was covered in flowers. Butterflies were scattered all over, gently fluttering their wings. How they got them to stay like that was a trick only the fae knew.

The dour looking officiant welcomed them. She probably still hadn't forgiven them for being so unruly during the rehearsal. It wasn't their fault Quinn was having mini episodes and her gargoyle wings kept popping out and trying to lift her off the ground which kept making everyone laugh. They eventually tied a rope from her to a tree to keep her still.

Stacy nodded at a small orchestra off to the side to begin playing. At the back, they could see Quinn and Tallie standing next to each other. They looked all grown up in their gowns and their hair done. He could already see he was going to have to set some dating ground rules. Maybe some kind of application for the guys to fill out before they're allowed to date the girls.

They floated down the aisle and took their places across from Maddox and Tristan. The music changed as everyone stood.

Tears filled Maddox's eyes as Marta came into view. She was so happy she was glowing. She looked like a princess in her ice blue gown. She only had eyes for Silas. As she walked toward them, her gaze never broke from his. When she stopped next to him, she let out a soft giggle.

Maddox's heart was melting. He'd never seen her so happy.

He reached over and grabbed Tristan's hand. His emotions were threatening to overwhelm him and he needed Tristan's touch to ground him.

The garden was silent as they said their vows. When they were announced as husband and wife, the crowd erupted. The butterflies all took off at once as they kissed. Gotta give it to the fae. They knew how to make things look magical.

Maddox grabbed Tristan's arm. "Hang back a second."

They smiled and nodded as they waited for everyone to file into the tent for the reception. When they were finally alone, Tristan lifted an eyebrow. "I love when you want to spend some alone time together, but this might not be the time or the place."

Sweat poured down Maddox's face.

Tristan's smile faded. "Are you okay?"

Maddox nodded, then got down on one knee. "I didn't have this planned, so I don't have a ring for you, but it just feels right. I fell for you the day I met you. I tried to fight it. I wasn't interested in a serious relationship and definitely not with someone that had been human a couple of weeks earlier. But you changed me. You showed me love, acceptance, and a whole lot of sass, and I love every bit of it. I want to marry you and raise a family with you. I know this may be too soon, but I have to do it. Tristan James, will you marry me?"

Tristan's jaw dropped as he stared down at Maddox. "Holy fucking shit, I didn't see this coming. But yes, hell fucking yes, I'll marry your crazy ass. I love you so much it hurts and nothing would make me happier than for the world to know you belong to me."

Screeches of excitement pierced the air. Maddox hadn't noticed Tallie and Quinn hiding at the end of the aisle.

They ran for them and tackled them each in a hug.

"When I saw you guys weren't following, I knew something was up." Tallie squealed. "I'm so happy."

The girls swapped and hugged the other guy. Quinn wiped a tear from her face. "Now that we know what we're doing, your wedding is going to be bigger and gayer and all around more awesome than this one!"

Tristan cringed as he looked at Maddox. "Would you consent to an elopement?"

The girls gasped like they'd been stabbed. Their voices of indignation melded together.

Maddox held his hands up. "He's kidding. Let's just keep this between us for now. Tonight is all about Silas and Marta. When they get back from their honeymoon, we'll share the good news."

Quinn hooked arms with Tallie as they headed back down the aisle. "I'm so glad we're staying with them while Silas and Marta are on their honeymoon. We'll have full access to plan the wedding with them. They won't be able to escape us."

They looked over their shoulders and smiled sweetly at Maddox and Tristan.

"Babe, I think maybe going into work tomorrow suddenly sounds like a really, really good idea." Tristan mock whispered.

Maddox didn't care where he was tomorrow as long as he was with Tristan. For the rest of his days, he wanted to be by his side, through thick and thin.

CHAPTER
Thirty-Six

THEY WALKED into the office on Monday morning, excited to be there and out of the house. Who knew having two teenagers in the house would be so exhausting?

"There they are," Raelle called out when they entered the pod. "Guys, the new parents have finally arrived."

"Oh hell no," Tristan grumbled as he looked from smiling face to smiling face.

Maddox walked to the front of the table, where Vic normally sat. "There is nothing you guys can say to ruin our good moods. As of Saturday night, Tristan has agreed to marry me." He gave them a huge, toothy smile.

Cheers went up as they pounced on them. Vic

slapped Maddox on the back. "I was at the wedding and you couldn't have given me the heads up?"

Maddox shrugged. "I can't believe Tallie and Quinn managed to keep it a secret."

Vic's jaw dropped. "They knew before me?"

Tristan chuckled. "We didn't tell them they hid and spied on us. They will make outstanding agents one day."

"Half the population of Tampa is going to weep when they hear the news that Maddox is off the market," Raelle called out with a wink.

Nothing could take the smile off Maddox's face. "Don't worry. The other half still has you." He winked at her.

Vic smiled, "We can celebrate later, but right now we need to get back to work. Sabrina has given me an update. They worked all weekend to get us this information so quickly. So if you see them, make sure you thank them and don't give them shit if they're grumpy."

"Except Bruce," Tristan called out, "He's always a grumpy ass, so it's nothing new."

Vic raised his hand to stall any bickering between Ensley and Tristan could start, "Sabrina and her team have successfully identified a number of the bodies. While they are still working on a few, it's now confirmed that at least three-quarters of our missing persons have been accounted for. Along with others, who she believes to have been homeless."

Sheppard whistled, "I'm going to go out on a limb and say that there's a good chance that most if not all of our still unaccounted for missing will be found as she progresses."

Vic nodded. "I believe so, yes. And it gets worse, I'm afraid." He paused as he looked around at the team. "Her preliminary findings are that the bodies are missing organs that are specific to their supernatural group or that can provide a unique benefit to humans."

Tristan blew out a breath. "Are you telling me they are trying to create more people like Quinn?"

"It's looking that way, yes." Vic agreed, "I asked Cole to look into the possibility of a black market opening here in our area and he discovered one started about four months ago. Once I received Sabrina's report, I had Cole check to see if supernatural organs were being sold out of there." He gestured for Cole to take over.

"So, the basic answer is yes. For a hefty price, you can procure a specific body part, or you can take what's on offer at any given time. The demand is far exceeding the supply at the moment, though."

Jaylen stared at Cole in shock. "Do you ever sleep?"

Cole smirked. "I'm not giving away any secrets as to how I manage all this in front of the boss."

Tristan chuckled as he saw the glare Vic gave the other man.

"On that note, here's your laptop back." Cole slid it across the table to Tristan. "Since I had it, I checked and your guy was meeting up with a ghost. The man doesn't exist, and the account has since been deleted."

"Well, that's what we expected." Tristan sighed as he grabbed the laptop. "All of the missing met with a ghost, right?"

Vic nodded. "I guess we found our connection, but the question is, how do we catch a ghost?"

"Hey, Tristan." Reed called out slowly as he shot a worried look at Maddox, "You remember how you were only one of two phoenixes in the area, and now the other one is dead…"

Maddox slammed his fist on the table. "Don't you fucking say it."

Reed winced and held up his hands as if to say

he surrendered. "I'm just saying, it's a surefire way to draw the perp out."

Vic scowled as he studied Tristan. "I hate to say it, but he's right. The question is, how do we get you on his radar?"

Jaylen raised his hand. "We just have to put an order in for something only he could give us. Then when the asshole comes for Tristan, we take him down."

Tristan nodded as he thought it over. "I'm willing to be bait. Who's going to be the buyers? It has to be you guys as humans, otherwise the game would be up before it began."

"I'll do it." Jaylen offered without hesitation.

"Not alone, you're not." Vic growled, "I'm not putting two of my agents at risk if it can be helped."

Lexi leaned forward so she could get Vic's attention. "I'll act as his wife and go with him."

Maddox's hands were fisted in his lap. "None of them are doing this without at least two kinds of trackers on them. Cell phones seem to easily disappear around this guy and I want to know where all of them are at all times."

Cole nodded. "We can do that. Our techs have some of the most sophisticated gadgets out there. I'll work on setting up a meet with the black market guy and also create fake socials for Tristan."

Tristan stood up, "Okay, but can I get a cool name, please?"

Cole laughed. "Yeah, I think I can arrange that. I'll also need some pictures to post that show proof you're a phoenix."

Maddox stood and grabbed Tristan's hand, "Come on, you haven't let your wings out since you were shot. Let's go up to the roof and see how it goes." He turned to the group. "Any of you want to come take some pictures while we fly around?"

"Fuck yeah," Derek called out as he jumped to his feet. "I didn't really get to see you when we were at the stadium, and I've gotta admit I'm really curious about your wings."

Tristan was sitting in his office, going through his new social media accounts. "You know, these make me seem like a really interesting guy."

Josh laughed, "So Cole is good at bullshit, is what you're saying?"

"Asshole," Tristan laughed as Cole called out that he'd gotten a reply.

They all moved into the pod to hear the details as Maddox moved to his side and laced their fingers together.

"This was a lot quicker than I expected. I'm not sure if that should be a red flag or not, but they've agreed to meet up with our prospective buyers tonight at eight pm at Armature Works." Cole recited as he read the message aloud. "They want us to go to the Astro Craft Ice Cream and order the Tampa Guava Cream Cheese Ice Cream and have a seat by the windows."

Vic absently tapped his fingers on the desk as he listened. "And we're sure this is legitimate?"

Cole shrugged. "As much as I can be. I built a solid background on both Jaylen and Lexi. Unless this guy is a better hacker than me, he won't find anything amiss. He checked their histories, credit reports and even pinged the bank account I set up to confirm it was all legitimate."

Tristan bit his lip as he listened. "So what do you need me to do?"

"You need to just go act like a normal guy. Post shit on your social media accounts, have fun, and be available. As you probably saw, your occupation is listed as a flying teacher."

Cole winked as the group chuckled at Tristan's expense.

"Really? I used to like you."

"It's reasonable," Cole joked. "They don't have to know you can't land yet. We'll keep that our secret.

"Fucking bastard." Tristan shook his head with a smile, "With friends like you who needs enemies."

Cole grinned. "They'll make contact pretty quickly if we give them enough incentive, which we will do." Cole passed a sheet of paper to Jaylen and Lexi. "I've given them the basic information that you're looking for a phoenix heart in the hopes it'll save Lexi's twin. I've also promised a handsome bonus if they can make this happen within the next couple of days, as time is limited for your sibling."

"That wouldn't actually work, though, right?" Lexi asked.

Every paranormal shrugged.

"It's all fringe science. Six months ago, this wasn't even a thing, but after Quinn's case, people started figuring it out. You hear about botched illegal surgeries all the time because they thought something might work without understanding how it all worked." Cole explained.

CHAPTER
Thirty-Seven

MADDOX HATED SITTING in the surveillance van. He wanted to be in the field, risking his life. Humans were so fragile and they were putting them in a seriously dangerous situation.

Josh's voice came over the earpiece. "Lexi and Jaylen have purchased the ice cream and gone to sit by the windows."

Everyone sat in tense silence as the minutes ticked by.

Willow chimed in. "A man is approaching them. He's got on blue jeans, a Tampa Bay Rays t-shirt, and a hat hiding most of his face."

Maddox really hated that she was already back in the field after the riot the previous week.

"Contact has been made. The man is doing most

of the talking. Jaylen has passed off the envelope with the deposit."

"We're on the move. Josh is going to follow the man from the right, and I'll follow from the left."

"No, don't split up." Vic cursed.

A few minutes later, Josh and Lexi were back at the van. "The guy is good. I lost him in the crowd."

Willow nodded. "I thought I had eyes on him and then he just disappeared."

"Just because he's human doesn't mean he isn't slick."

Jaylen and Lexi walked up behind them. Jaylen handed back another envelope of money. "Dude is creepy. He sounded knowledgeable, like he has some kind of medical training. He was very convincing. If I were desperate for a cure, I would believe anything he tried to sell me. He did warn us, though, that it is new science, so there is no guarantee. He did try to push us toward a lion heart, but we insisted we heard about a successful transplant in another state from a phoenix and were only interested in that. I only had to give him a deposit. We give the rest when he delivers the organ."

"Okay. We made it over the first hurdle. Now we wait to see if the guy takes the bait and reaches out to Tristan. Keep your phones on you at all times. If a meet is set up, I want everyone ready to go." Vic waited for each person to nod. "Okay. Go get some sleep. We have a medical murderer to catch."

Maddox couldn't take five steps away from Tristan. He felt like at any moment he would disappear. It wasn't rational, and it wasn't fair to Tristan. He was a federal agent and a damn good one, but that didn't make Maddox's fear of losing him any better.

"You're staring again." Tristan mumbled without looking up from the report he was typing up.

Cole rushed into the office. "You got a hit. Get on Facebook. He responded to your ad for flying lessons."

Maddox took a deep breath before he got up and stood over Tristan's shoulder.

Tristan logged in and opened the messenger section. In bold letters was a message request from Daniel Wilson.

'Hello - I saw your ad for flying lessons. My son is desperate to fly. I don't have that ability as my wife was the one with wings.'

A picture of a man with a boy around ten was attached.

Jaylen pushed between them to look at the screen. "That's not the guy we met with."

The message went on. "I homeschool my son so we are very flexible on when we can meet. I saw your references, you come highly recommended. You can call me at 813-472-4857 to set up a day and time that works for you."

Jasmina snorted. "He doesn't sound like a crazy killer at all. He even has a nice family photo."

"That's because he's not crazy. This is a business transaction for him." Maddox said through gritted teeth.

Tristan blew out a breath. "Okay, how do I respond?"

"Let's give him a call and tell him you can meet him at Cypress Point Park," Vic offered.

The room was silent as Tristan put his cell phone on speaker and dialed the number.

"Hello?"

"Hi, this is Bryce Walken. I received your message about the flying lessons for your son."

"Oh great. Thank you for getting back to me so quickly. We're new to the area, so when my son Danny Junior asked for flying lessons, I was at a loss. I was so lucky to stumble upon your ad."

Tristan forced out a laugh. "I'm glad you did. I've

been doing this for a long time, so your son will be in excellent hands. I can meet at five o'clock today or tomorrow at Cypress Point Park if that works for Danny's schedule?"

"Hmmm, you know, your references are great, but I'm still nervous about letting a complete stranger fly off with my son. Is it okay if you and I meet first, then we can set up the first lesson?"

Tristan glanced at the rest of the agents and rolled his eyes. "I totally get it. I don't blame you for wanting to be safe. Where did you have in mind?"

"There's a tavern near the St. Pete Pier called The Two Crows. I can be there at seven tonight if that works for you?"

Vic gave Tristan a thumbs up. "Sounds good. See you tonight."

Tristan hit the end button as everyone in the room let out a tense breath at the same time.

"Okay, let's pull up a map of the area and plan where everyone will be stationed."

Maddox sat at the bar of the Two Crows sipping on a whiskey. The place had filled up at six thirty when a live band had started playing. It was loud and crowded. Not a great place for a sting.

At seven on the dot, Tristan walked in and went to the other end of the bar. A few minutes later, a man at a table by the bathrooms stood up and called his name.

Maddox watched as Tristan walked over and shook hands with the guy.

Cole came across the earpiece. "Jaylen, Lexi, I'm sending the guy's picture your way."

A second later, Lexi responded. "That's not the guy we met with."

"Great, that means there are multiple people involved." Vic cursed.

Maddox scanned the bar, trying to see if anyone else stood out like they were there with Daniel.

Maddox turned around on his bar stool to face the room. He rocked back and forth to the music.

The song built until everyone was on their feet dancing. Maddox moved further down the bar to not lose sight of Tristan, but when he got around the crowd, the table was empty.

Maddox pushed past the bile rising in his throat. "He's gone. Everyone get here now. Cole, what's his tracker say?"

Several people were talking at once. "Everyone stop talking except Cole." Maddox roared.

Vic and Reed got to Maddox's position first. They'd been stationed outside the front entrance. "They didn't go out the front."

Jasmina came in from the back. "No one went out the back door."

Finally, Cole spoke. "The tracker says he's still there."

The rest of the team had gathered. They split up and searched the bathrooms, storage rooms, and under every table. Maddox was doing everything he could not to panic.

Cole was at the bar, staring at a laptop. "Wait, he's on the move. He's heading down the pier."

Everyone took off, with Maddox leading the way. He didn't care who he had to shove. Kiely shifted and took off in the air to scout from above.

Sheppard ran ahead and made it back to them before they were even at the entrance of the pier. "I didn't see Tristan or our target. I don't smell him either."

Cole shoved past them. "It still shows him at the end of the pier. Come on."

They waved their badges, but security stopped

them. "This is a human day. You can't be here until tomorrow."

"Fuck you. Let us in." Maddox growled.

Vic stepped in front of him and spoke to the scared man staring up at Maddox. "We are tracking someone who is in danger. Our intel says he's in there. Let us go."

"Kiely, his tracker is moving across the water." Cole relayed into the mic.

The head of security came up and, after a heated argument with Vic, agreed to let them through with an escort.

They rushed to the end and looked over the edge. In the distance, several boats were going different directions.

Kiely finally replied. "I have a bunch of scared humans wondering why I'm on their boat. The guy from the bar isn't here. Either is the guy Jaylen and Lexi met with. I'm going to move on to the next boat, but there's quite a few."

Maddox leaped from the pier and took off in the direction they had disappeared into.

"Cole, talk to me. Are they still moving?"

"Yeah, he's going fast, so he has to still be on the water."

Maddox and Kiely went from boat to boat, checking the occupants.

Maddox growled. "None of these are the guy."

"It stopped. Head toward the shoreline." Cole instructed.

"Where? There are boats docked everywhere."

"The tracker has shifted a little onshore but hasn't moved. I'll text you the coordinates. We're going to drive over there."

Maddox stopped flying long enough to get the coordinates and put them in the GPS of his phone. He whistled at Kiely to follow him and led her toward a cluster of warehouses.

They landed and Kiely immediately shifted. "Cole, can you narrow this down at all? There are several buildings, and they all have at least seven stories."

"The map just says unit F. We're ten minutes out."

"Fuck." Maddox roared into the night. The sound echoed through the empty parking lots.

Kiely grabbed him and shook him. "You take that building and I'll take this one."

He nodded and ran to his right. He barreled through the locked doors and ignored the pain that shot through his shoulder. "The first floor is labeled Unit A."

"Mine does too. So they must be floors and not buildings. I'm going up," Kiely replied.

Maddox ran through the floor and finally found the stairs in the back corner. As he ran up each flight, he passed signs for units B, C, D, E, and finally F on the sixth floor. He pulled out his gun and went in. Tristan had to be there. Maddox didn't know what to do if he wasn't.

CHAPTER
Thirty-Eight

THE FLOOR WAS silent except for the sound of Maddox's rapid breathing. He wasn't out of breath, he was panicked.

"This unit F is clear." Kiely said. "I'm heading to the next building."

Maddox focused on his unit. He methodically went through until he'd cleared the entire floor. "Mine's clear too."

He busted out a window and leaped from it. He flew to the roof of the next building and had to break through the door to get inside. He could hear sirens coming closer. Soon the entire team would be there and then Maddox wouldn't feel so alone and out of control.

He ran down the stairs and passed the seventh

floor, unit G, and kept going. He stopped at unit F and slipped through the door. At first, he didn't hear anything, but as he got further across the floor, he could hear quiet murmuring.

"I think I found them." He whispered into his mic.

"We're pulling up. Wait for backup." Vic ordered.

There was no way Maddox was going to comply. Vic could fire him later for it.

A small stream of light was coming through under a door near the end.

He took a deep breath and kicked the door in. "Freeze."

Tristan was strapped to a table, unconscious, while a man stood over him. He looked shocked to see Maddox standing there.

"Step away and I won't kill you," Maddox warned.

Blue and red lights were shining through the windows. The man looked around in a panic, then took his scalpel and stabbed it straight into Tristan's heart. He twisted it as the bullet from Maddox's gun hit him.

Maddox roared as he saw Tristan's eyes go wide. He bucked off the table as much as the straps would allow, then went still.

Maddox got to the man, who was holding his shoulder where the bullet wound was.

"You won't be able to help him. I shredded his heart. You weren't fast enough. Add him to the list of people you didn't save."

Maddox saw red. He grabbed the man and squeezed. He didn't care that the man was screaming or that he could hear bones snapping. He wanted him to hurt as much as Maddox was hurting at that moment.

Kiely screamed his name and pulled on his arm. "Maddox. Go to Tristan. I got this."

He snapped out of his haze and dropped the man on the floor. Tristan was so pale under the surgical light. As long as Maddox lived, he'd never forget the red of Tristan's shirt as blood spread across him.

He stepped near to check him but pulled back when Tristan went up in flames. One second he was lying there still and the next he was an inferno.

Maddox felt people pulling on him. Vic smacked him across the face. "Maddox enough. Get back."

He couldn't comprehend what he was being told. How could they expect him to move away from the love of his life?

The fire was out in minutes. All that was left behind was ash and smoke.

Sheppard was holding Willow as she sobbed in his arms.

Maddox was briefly aware of Cole on his knees staring at the now empty table.

Vic was on the phone shouting at someone. Time stood still as chaos went on all around him.

He vaguely saw more agents arrive. Logan had tried to go to him, but Finneas held him back.

Maddox couldn't move. He was numb.

Someone tried pulling Maddox over to a chair, but he was stuck. Tristan wasn't leaving. How could he?

"I need something to take him with me." He finally glanced around at the faces staring back at him. "I can't leave him. Do we have something I can use?"

Reed punched a hole through the wall and stormed out.

Ensley walked up and grabbed his hands. "We'll get you something. You don't have to go anywhere."

A roar rushed through the room. Air gusted, sending papers and medical supplies flying.

The ashes on the table lifted with the wind into a

tornado. Everyone covered their faces to hide from the biting wind, but Maddox couldn't look away.

The ashes spun faster and faster as flames of fire sparked from them until they burst and Tristan lay there.

The room went still. It took a few seconds before anyone moved. Vic reached out to check Tristan's neck for a pulse when Tristan gasped and sat up.

Vic nearly fell backward, but Cross caught him.

Maddox ran for Tristan and pulled him into his arms. It didn't matter that they were surrounded by co-workers. Maddox sobbed in his arms.

Tristan grabbed Maddox's head and made him look at him. "Hey, what's all this? What's wrong?"

Ensley walked up with a big smile on her face. "Dude, you died. You burst into flames, then you were a dust tornado, and here you are. Best dead body ever."

Her joke broke the tension in the room.

Maddox held onto Tristan and continued sobbing.

"Come on, let's give them a minute," Vic ordered.

After a few minutes of Tristan rubbing Maddox's back, he tried again to pull Maddox up to look at him. "Babe. It's okay. I don't know what the hell

Ensley was talking about, but it doesn't matter. I'm here. You can stop. I'm okay."

"Don't you ever do that to me again. You don't get to die first. You are mine. I'm keeping you until the day I die. You hear me? I don't care if phoenixes can be reborn or whatever you call it. Don't ever do that to me again."

Maddox was still shaking as he helped Tristan down from the table. "Where are we?"

Maddox gave him a watery laugh. "Come on. We have a lot to talk about."

Thirty~Nine

TRISTAN SAT AT THE TABLE, trying to ignore the stares of his teammates. After self-combusting two nights earlier, he'd been sent to Shifter General where Dr Obinski and most of the staff were stunned to hear about his rebirth. Apparently, the lore around his kind wasn't well known since they were so rare. Just what Tristan wanted, to be another first to do something.

Dr Obinski had declared him in perfect health and against Maddox's objection, he sent him home after one night of observation.

Silas and Marta had cut their honeymoon short when they'd heard what happened and now they were camped out at Maddox's and his apartment because Marta said she wasn't ready to let him out of her sight. It was a battle to get her to agree to let him go into the office.

Vic had offered to let Tristan have as much time off as he wanted, but why? Tristan felt better than he had in years.

Now his team was staring at him with mixed looks of curiosity, awe, and guilt. Both Reed and Cole had taken his death personally and still hadn't forgiven themselves for their part in it.

Tristan had no hard feelings toward anyone. They were doing a job and had done it to the best of their abilities. They stopped the man responsible and hopefully saved future paranormals.

Vic laid a file on the table and sat down. "I've read the full report, but I know many of you haven't, so I thought it would be best if we recap all together." He flipped open the file. "Tristan reported he was speaking with the man Daniel when a spray was aimed at his face. He vaguely remembered getting shoved into some kind of box as he was losing consciousness. On the boat, we found a box on wheels with the band's name on it from the bar. After genetic testing of Daniel, it was determined he was a shapeshifter named Henry Nelson. He was likely the same person at every meeting. Here's where it gets really crazy." Tristan couldn't imagine how it could get any crazier. "We've been doing some digging and found shell companies owned the landfill where the bodies were dumped and the building where Tristan was taken to. Cole traced those shell companies back to another shell corporation that he is continuing to look into."

Tristan's jaw dropped. "So we didn't stop it with Daniel? There's someone bigger out there? I died for nothing?" Maddox glared at him. He shrugged. "I was just teasing."

"It's not funny. I'm not ready for you to joke about it." Maddox answered sadly.

Tristan squeezed his thigh. "I'm sorry. You're right." He'd heard stories from everyone that had been in the room on how everything had gone down, and still he couldn't imagine what Maddox felt in those moments. It had to be torture. The fact that Maddox had woken up screaming several times proved he was still having nightmares about it.

Vic closed the file in front of him. "We still have a lot to do here. We're not stopping now. We'll find this shell corporation and hold them responsible. My out of town guests are still a problem too. But if anyone can solve these problems, it's this task force. I am damn lucky to have you all on my team."

The End

Maddox, Tristan, and the whole gang will be back soon. Who's behind the rift kidnappings? Who is the mystery shell corporation? It's never a dull moment with the Agents of the Paranormal Investigative Services.

If you loved Faeted Under Fire, we have a special offer just for you. We will have a limited edition merch box available soon with a custom hardback version of the book. There will only be 50 made. If you want more information on when these merch boxes become available, you can follow Cassidy and Sheri on Facebook or join their newsletters.

Cassidy's Facebook:
www.facebook.com/cassidykoconnorauthor

Sheri's Facebook:
https://www.facebook.com/sheri.lyn.author

Cassidy's Newsletter:
https://www.subscribepage.com/cassidykoconnor

Sheri's Newsletter:
https://www.subscribepage.com/sherilyn

About the Authors

Cassidy lives in the Tampa, Florida area with her high school sweetheart, their three children, her dog Flynn who she loves obsessively, and her grand dog, Ryder. She loves reading and going to the movies. She also loves to travel and hopes to one day watch a baseball game in every MLB stadium in the country.

She also writes under the pen name C.K. O'Connor. Books by C.K. range from sweet romance to young adult to historical romance.

To learn more about C.K. / Cassidy please visit her online at

www.cassidykoconnor.com.

You can also find her on Facebook at

https://www.facebook.com/C.K.-OConnor-Author-101376192171379

OR

www.facebook.com/cassidykoconnorauthor

Hi, I'm Sheri Lyn. I live in Florida with the two loves of my life, my dog's Bailey and Boone. I love living here and couldn't imagine living anywhere else.

I'm an avid reader who kept dreaming of a story that wanted to be told and that's where my first book was born.

When I'm not reading or proofing, I'm at the evil day job where my sanity is tested on a daily basis. My sarcastic quips can provide a much-needed break until I can return home to my puppies and books, my joys in life.

Please visit my website to keep up with my books and to sign up for my newsletter for excerpts, give-aways and fun.

Sherilynauthor.com and on Twitter - @sherilynauthor